The Boarding School Series: Book 2

The Duke's Blackmailed Bride

Elizabeth Lennox

The series includes five books, plus a collection of introduction stories. The introduction stories are available in the first book's paperback edition, as well as free online from the website.

CONTENTS

Prologue

Three Years Ago....

Sierra Warner forced yet another smile of greeting as one more guest congratulated her. "Thank you. It is indeed very exciting," she lied.

Lie? Sierra tilted her head as the person said something, but her thoughts dwelled on her state of mind. Why did she think accepting congratulations was a lie? She was getting married! She should be excited.

She supposed, in a strange way, she was thrilled to be marrying Evan. He was handsome and intelligent – an up and coming investment broker with her father's firm – everything she should want in a husband. At least, that's what her mother told her. All the time. Every time she crossed paths with her mother, Sierra heard how lucky she was to be marrying so well and that Evan was going to be a very good provider, an excellent husband.

So why was she avoiding her mother lately? And why did the thought of Evan touching any part of her body make her...nauseous?

That was ridiculous, she told herself firmly. His touch didn't make her sick! She was just nervous. Evan was a good man. A kind man. If the sparks were missing any time he touched her or kissed her, well, perhaps the romance novels she loved so much had set unrealistic expectations for her.

Sierra sighed and forced her mind to focus on the current conversation. Evan was one of the good guys, she reminded herself. He treated her with great respect, and was very attentive to all of her wishes. If she even hinted that she wanted something, he went out and bought it for her. It had gotten so bad lately that she'd learned to be careful with her words, not wanting him to buy her any more trinkets.

She glanced down at the diamond ring on her finger, noting how the light sparkled against the enormous center stone. It was an extremely large diamond. Not really her style, but she supposed she would get used to it. It felt very heavy, she thought, and everyone seemed to be dazzled by the stone. Sierra felt like she was being ridiculous to be wishing for a smaller diamond, perhaps something a bit less…ostentatious. She was just being silly. Diamonds were…a status symbol, she thought and quickly smothered her spurt of resentment.

But as she looked around at the guests, everyone laughing and chatting, drinking and eating, she realized that she was right on target. Looking at Evan, she actually had to smother a spurt of revulsion. This diamond was not a reflection of Evan's love for her, she suddenly realized. The man couldn't love her. He didn't even know her! This ridiculously large and pretentious diamond ring was a symbol of his power, or what he hoped his power would be, she thought.

And at the same time, why should she feel slighted or even indignant? She didn't really know Evan either. They were basically strangers who had gone out on a few dates and, strangely, ended up engaged.

So why was she marrying the man? Why was she standing here in her parents' elegantly decorated living room, surrounded by her father's friends, coworkers and clients, listening to their congratulations?

Sierra had no idea! She had no idea what she was doing and, even more pathetically, she didn't know why she was marrying a man she didn't truly know or love.

She sighed as she smiled yet again and showed one more person her engagement ring, acting as if the thoughts running through her mind weren't rebellious and crazy. Yes, she was happy. Yes, she was thrilled to be marrying someone with such a great future. Yes, Evan was very intelligent. Yes…she continued to agree with everything everyone said about Evan.

Although….

Her heart wasn't in it.

As he stood next to her and held his arm around her waist, Sierra looked up at the man, traitorous thoughts swimming through her mind but she shook her head, ruthlessly smothered the negativity, thinking she was just being silly and anxious over a major life change. Of course this would be a solid marriage, she told herself. She was just going through normal doubts about her decision to marry. These were just nerves. She felt an affection for Evan. He was a good man. He was kind and considerate. A woman could do a lot worse for herself, she thought.

Although…she couldn't help wondering if there was more.

Mentally shaking her head as the doorbell rang once again, Sierra told herself that she was just being ungrateful. More of Evan's university mates, she realized with a resigned sigh as she pasted a bright smile on her face. Evan stepped away, embracing the newcomers with a hard slap and more ribald teasing. She didn't understand half of their humor because so much of it referred to jokes from their school days. Sierra hadn't gone to university, but she would have loved to attend.

Why hadn't that thought occurred to her before now? And why hadn't she gone to university after high school? Maybe because none of her friends had?

She'd simply attended finishing school with them. She could seat an entire banquet of diplomats and aristocrats with ease, perform an elegant waltz, or hold a prolonged conversation in French.

How were those skills relevant in today's society, she suddenly asked herself? Why had she done this to her life? Why hadn't she followed her dreams? Why hadn't she eschewed her friends' path and gone her own way, made something of herself?

Shaking her head, she mentally pulled herself back to the present and admonished herself for her ridiculous thoughts. She was just nervous. Becoming engaged was a huge milestone and she was anxious about stepping into the role of a society wife with Evan.

Besides, she was twenty years old now. It was too late for her to attend university. She looked up at Evan and suddenly noticed that he had a weak chin. Was that important? Should she care? He had a good mind, what did a chin matter? In the grand scheme of things, should she even be looking at the man's chin? Was she being superficial?

And what about her desires to go to university? Why was it too late? She'd always wanted to care for animals. Maybe she still could, she thought even as she also noticed that Evan reminded her of a bloodhound. Especially around the eyes. And the mouth. She'd never really looked at his mouth before. Their kisses hadn't been extremely passionate. Usually a simple kiss on the cheek.

Was that significant as well?

Sierra's mouth twisted as she pushed all of these issues aside. She was marrying the man. She'd made her decision, her life was planned out.

Although...university would have been fascinating! Yes, she could have truly thrived in an environment of higher learning. Too bad her chance for attending was gone.

Wasn't it?

She sighed and quickly ducked when Evan's elbow almost chucked her on the chin. She was getting pretty good tonight! That was the second time he'd almost knocked her. A less confident woman might think he was aiming for her head.

Evan's enthusiasm for his university chums was surprising since, normally, Evan was relatively calm and composed. He adhered to all the rules of etiquette and expected her to do the same so it was very strange to see him so...boisterous!

She glanced across the room at her father and noticed his chagrin. Obviously, he had noticed Evan's near miss at her head and his overly enthusiastic greetings towards his school buddies. Perhaps it might be time to rein Evan back in. "Honey," she said, gently tapping his shoulder. Once again, she had to move quickly out of the way of Evan's swinging arm or he would have knocked her out.

He only turned when three of his friends looked at her as if she'd committed a crime by interrupting their excitement.

Evan was quick to recover though and that meant something, didn't it?

"Oh, honey!" he said, finally remembering that she was by his side – and why. His hands came out to steady her. "I'm so sorry, love." He chuckled, obviously more than a little drunk. "Good moves, though, honey!" Sierra noticed that he'd kept his glass of scotch safe even if he'd just about knocked her out with his wild flailing.

Sierra's younger brother, Daniel, almost tripped into the foyer. "Yeah, sis, good moves ducking from your fiancée's wayward fists."

Sierra thought that Daniel's words were a bit harsh for his age. He was only fifteen years old. Shouldn't he be with his own friends about now instead of hanging out with the older guys who were drinking heavily? He was too young to be chumming around with Evan's friends, wasn't he?

"Are you okay?" Evan asked, appearing solicitous and concerned.

"Yes," she said even as she smoothed her hands down her chiffon skirt and ignored her brother. He was still a teen, eager to join in with the big boys in Evan's group. "I think that perhaps we should mingle among the other guests," she pointed out, her eyes drifting pointedly to her father who was not amused by Evan's immature antics.

Evan looked over to where his boss was standing with the other partners on either side of him; Sierra's father looking disapproving. He stiffened up and pulled away from his friends, cleared his throat and nodded with as much dignity as he could while still inebriated. "Right," and he pulled her against his side a bit too roughly for her taste, but she laid a hand on his chest to steady herself and regain her balance. "Too tight, Evan," she whispered under her breath.

He rolled his eyes, but he loosened his grip. "Wouldn't want to harm the princess, now would I?"

Sierra didn't like his sarcasm, but she wasn't going to call him out at the moment. That was a conversation for later, and one that she truly needed to have with him. His comments had been a bit too patronizing lately and she didn't like it. Why hadn't she said something before now? Why was she accepting that kind of tone and those belittling words? "Let's go say hello to Patrick, your soon-to-be boss," she suggested even as she smiled up at him, trying to appear undisturbed by his derision.

Patrick was one of her father's partners in the investment firm, as well as a good friend. They were part of the group on the other side of the living room. Evan sighed, looking a bit petulant for a moment. "I guess that's what I should do, shouldn't I?" he replied.

Sierra couldn't believe that he was even asking the question. Evan was the one who had insisted on this night and had even insisted on the guest list. After he'd slid the ring on her finger and announced that they would be married, she'd urged him to hold off for a few more weeks to have the engagement party. But since she hadn't been able to give him a reason why, he'd ignored her desires to hold off. So now he had to deal with his guests. "Yes, it is the polite thing to do," she explained with as much patience as she could muster. "Your tie is askew."

Evan immediately fixed his tie, roughly pulled her once again against his side and nodded his head. "Okay, lead the way, princess."

Sierra was really starting to hate that nickname. When he'd first used it, she'd assumed he was putting her on a pedestal and she hadn't liked it then. Now, the nickname seemed more sarcastic or just plain mean, as if he were pointing out that she was a snob in some way. Or that she required special attention that he was obligated to give her but didn't like to.

She didn't feel like a snob, she thought as she moved around the room, introducing Evan to her father's friends and associates. She just knew what was appropriate during an important social gathering. Her mother had been good at helping her father's career by entertaining coworkers, clients and potential clients over the years. They'd had a strong alliance and, if her parents didn't seem extremely happy together, at least they both had found a degree of satisfaction in their own hobbies. Her father was an avid fisherman who liked to take long weekends and hide out near a stream somewhere in the wilderness. He rarely caught any fish and, whatever he did catch, he threw back, not wanting to carry the fish home or, even worse, clean and gut the fish. He just liked being in the outdoors.

Her mother, on the other hand, eschewed all outdoor activities, thinking they were uncivilized. She had all of her charities that occupied her time and she enjoyed long lunches with her friends, all of whom were within the same socio-economic level as she was and, therefore, deemed "appropriate" friends.

Sierra suddenly realized that her friends were extremely similar to her mother's. Why did that realization bother her so much? Looking over at her small cluster of friends, she wondered why she was suddenly disturbed by their presence. They were all acting perfectly acceptably, laughing at all the correct moments, sharing the appropriately humorous stories, gossiping about…everything and everyone. Had she done that? Does she look just as…fake…when she's sitting with that group?

Glancing back at her parents, both of whom were standing together but not touching, she knew that their relationship was none of her business. It was a marriage that seemed to work for both of them. Sierra just hoped she and Evan could work out an equally satisfying arrangement. She looked up at him as she introduced him to yet another of the important clients at the firm and she was proud of him. He'd slipped out of his college persona and was acting much more mature, more personable.

The doorbell rang once again but she gently tugged Evan over to another client that she had met a while ago, thinking the man and his wife would be a useful contact for Evan at some point. The housekeeper would open the door to the late arrival and ensure that the guest received a drink quickly. It wasn't until they were close to Patrick and her father that she felt an odd sensation but she ignored it, thinking it was just her imagination. Patrick and Evan were discussing something and she scanned the room, trying to decide if there was someone else that Evan should speak with.

That was when her eyes caught sight of him.

He was at least a head taller than the others in the room. And she noticed that there was something else about him, something that she couldn't really define but the undefinable quality dramatically set him apart from the other guests.

Perhaps it was just his confidence, she thought. Or maybe it was the fact that he was extremely good looking. Or his broad, fascinating shoulders?

She wasn't quite sure. All she knew was that she couldn't look away from him. That compelling quality sliced through the air, making her heart rate pick up and her breath catch in her throat. It was strange, she thought, but she wanted to push the other guests aside so that she could walk up to this man and simply stare at him.

And then his eyes caught hers! That compelling feeling switched off and in its place she felt a startling, shocking surge of electricity, a jolt of raw awareness. As she stared at the man, as his eyes held hers in a captive assault on her senses, she felt like she was his prisoner. It actually made her body ache in some scandalous way that she didn't understand. And definitely didn't like!

She tried to look away. She reached up to touch Evan's arm, wanting to hide behind him. But Evan was only a couple of inches taller than she was and the new man's dangerously compelling eyes told her that he wasn't going to release her. Not just yet.

"Oh my goodness," her mother hissed.

Evan's eyes snapped over to where her mother was looking. Her father seemed bizarrely excited to see the man and Sierra suddenly had an uneasy feeling about the night. "Damn! I didn't think he'd show up!"

Even Patrick stiffened as the man in question stepped further into the room.

"He needs a drink" her mother eagerly commented, a peculiar, almost frantic quality to her voice that Sierra had never heard before. A moment later, her mother was gone, off to greet this stranger with the mysteriously dark eyes and jet-black hair, a hard, square jaw that made her want to smooth her hand over the edge and soothe out the indomitable aggression somehow.

"Do you know him?" Evan snapped.

Those words and, especially the tone, were so startling that it helped break the connection between the stranger's eyes and her body. She looked up at her fiancée, startled that he would sound so belligerent. "No. I've never met him before. Why do you ask?"

Evan was more than slightly irritated. "Because you're staring at him as if he's your next dessert. You're about to be married. Just remember that," he snapped and hauled her up against his side one more time, his fingers digging into the soft flesh of her waist and hurting her.

By that point, her mother had gotten the tall man a drink and had brought him over to their circle. "Everyone, I'm very pleased to introduce you to Harrison Aimsworth, Duke of Selton," she said with a quiver of excitement in her voice.

She felt Evan stiffen in surprise. In fact, everyone jerked a bit more upright and Sierra could have laughed at how everyone was so amazed to be in the presence of a duke that they reached for their tie and straightened their shoulders.

All Sierra wanted to do was hide behind the curtains. Especially when those midnight blue eyes slashed over to her grey ones and she felt herself shiver with an awareness that she felt right down to her toes. Her fingers, which had been trying to loosen Evan's grasp, froze and her whole body heated with the intensity of the man's gaze on her.

"This is my daughter, Sierra," her mother explained. "And her fiancée, Evan Winters."

The man greeted Evan first and they spent a moment discussing sports or stocks, she wasn't sure which since both topics sounded similar. She watched carefully, her whole body trembling, fearful of the moment when this stranger would turn to her. She didn't want to extend her hand, afraid of what his hand would feel like. She'd already experienced his eyes, she wasn't sure her body could handle his touch.

And then his attention sliced over to her and it was just as bad as that first gaze had been. "Ms. Warner," he greeted her. "I suppose congratulations are in order," the stranger said with a deep, sexy voice that seemed to vibrate throughout her entire body. And then he did it! The greeting that she'd been fearing from the moment he'd stepped into the house! Extending his hand, he took her smaller one in his. "It is a delight to meet you. Your father speaks very highly of you."

Sierra shivered as that visceral awareness sparked through her once again. Her lips felt numb even while the rest of her body felt like it was on fire, starting with her hand which was still in his warm, confident grip.

"Thank you very much, Your Grace," she replied. "It is an honor that you would attend our celebration."

"When is the wedding?" he asked, his eyes looking into hers and she swore that she saw amusement there. Or interest? She wasn't sure which. And neither made sense.

Besides, those blue eyes were making her nervous and…other feelings she couldn't really define. "Um…we haven't set a date yet. We're just…"

"It will be this summer," Evan announced out of the blue, causing her eyes to glance up to his. Her mouth fell open as she absorbed the impact of his announcement. A wedding in only a few months? Was he serious? "I just put the ring on her finger so we're working through the details." With that, he lifted Sierra's hand up, showing off her diamond ring.

Sierra felt as if she was on display and the size of her engagement ring denoted some sort of validation of Evan's virility. Was this more about measuring up? Wouldn't it be more direct to just lay one's penis out on the dining room table with a measuring tape?

Sierra silently laughed at the idea and she suspected that Evan would come up lacking in that department against this taller man.

She didn't really understand men, having spent more time with animals than humans. They made more sense, she thought.

She pulled her hand gently back down to her side and tried to think of something to say to the strange and intimidating man looking down at her. "We're delighted you could attend tonight. Was it difficult to find the house?" she asked, relying on tired conversational topics that were easy because her mind simply couldn't come up with anything more stimulating at the moment.

Harrison looked down at the beautiful woman and couldn't believe she was marrying such an ass. This delicate flower and this brash idiot of a fiancée just didn't fit. Why was she marrying a man who could barely handle his liquor?

"Your mother provided excellent directions. And the house is lovely. I'm sure the grounds are excellent as well."

Sierra's face brightened. "Oh, they're delightful during the springtime," she smiled, embracing an easy subject. "Do you ride?"

The man nodded slightly. "I love horses, although I don't get out as often as I'd like."

Her brother chose that moment to burst into their group, ignoring the tension as he wrapped his arm around Sierra's shoulders. "That's pretty much all my sister likes to do. Ride and take care of the ornery beasts," he teased. A moment later, he was gone again, more excited to sneak liquor behind their parent's back than to converse with important guests.

She blushed and glanced up at the enormous man, wondering if there was even a horse in the stables that could hold a man of his size. While she was a couple of inches shorter than Evan, this man towered over her and she stood up taller, not liking the feeling of being so small, so vulnerable. She'd never felt that way before and she fought against it now in this man's presence. She wasn't small!

"The roses are my mother's pride and joy," she finished lamely.

"Perhaps when the weather warms up, I'll come back and be able to enjoy them during the day."

Sierra was relieved when Patrick stepped in, taking over the conversation. She stepped back, needing space to regroup. Never, in all her years of entertaining with her mother, had she had trouble speaking with a guest. Her mother had taught her well but this man just did something to her, made her mind turn all mushy with crazy thoughts popping into her head. Crazy and inappropriate thoughts!

So why was she so flustered by this man's presence? Why did she feel like she needed to wipe her palms against her dress?

Sierra excused herself carefully and stepped into the kitchen, relieved to have some time alone. She stayed out of the way of the catering staff, but the whole time, she leaned against one of the cabinets, trying to get her heart rate back under control. This was crazy, she told herself! He was just a man! Evan was handsome and her father's features were very well put together. Even Patrick was a nice looking gentleman! None of them made her feel this...odd sensation. So what was it about this newcomer that had her so frazzled?

She peered out into the living room and realized that Evan, her father and Patrick had the man well entertained. But even as she peered out, he turned his head and caught her gaze. She felt her pulse leap with the impact of those eyes, startled that he'd known she was looking at him. Thankfully, the kitchen door swung closed once more, blocking his view and she turned and fled.

Sierra knew that she couldn't hide in the kitchen forever. But she stood in the warmth while the housekeeper, a kind woman named Ruth, supervised the catering staff, directing them all like a military general. The kitchen was a haven. Sierra had spent hours in here, doing her homework, chatting with Ruth while the robust housekeeper made dinners and breakfasts or just hiding from the cold indifference of the other members of the house. Her parents were rarely home in the afternoons, so Sierra had taken to just sitting at the scarred, wooden table, talking with Ruth most afternoons when she wasn't out riding. Ruth was a generous woman who laughed easily and was a genius at whipping up delicious meals.

Sierra stood in the warm, brightly lit kitchen for several moments, just until she felt more balanced. Ruth helped by walking by and patting her arm gently, almost as if the gentle woman knew that Sierra was feeling out of her depth.

Taking a deep breath, Sierra stepped back out into the main area once again, knowing that she had responsibilities as a hostess. But that didn't mean she was going back to Evan's side. She'd had enough of him for one night, she thought. She moved to the other side of the room, greeting guests, asking the wait staff to start watering down Evan's friends' drinks so he and his friends wouldn't become too rowdy and found her own group of friends clustered in the corner. She huddled there for a while, relieved to have a hiding place as well as a reprieve from Evan. And that man, she thought even as her eyes skimmed through the room. She kept an eye on him, knowing where he was at all times. It was only because he was obviously an important guest and had nothing to do with the way he intimidated her, she told herself firmly.

As she listened to her friends drone on about some party they'd attended the night before, a party which she'd left early, she couldn't really understand what was happening to her. Why should she need a reprieve from the man she was going to marry?

And because she didn't have an answer to that question, something else occurred to her. Why was she actually marrying Evan? She didn't love him. Her father had suggested that the two of them go out on a date. From there, she just sort of found herself engaged.

Evan hadn't even really proposed, she realized. Just one day, her father had asked if they had considered marriage. Evan had looked at her and said they'd already talked about it, ignoring Sierra's startled glance. The next day, he'd put a ring on her finger. That had been last week.

Glancing across the room, she spotted Evan, once again with a fresh drink in his hand and surrounded by his college buddies, laughing too loudly and generally just being obnoxious.

It suddenly occurred to her that she didn't really like Evan. They rarely had conversations, just the two of them. They'd gone out to dinner a couple of times, but mostly they attended social events together. That didn't really give them opportunities to talk with each other, discover commonalities and mutual interests.

How long had she been just floating along, she wondered? Why had she let her life get out of hand without questioning her future? And why in the world had she gone along with an engagement to a man she didn't even like?

It was one thing to not love him, she thought, startled as her mind began to unravel her relationship with Evan. It was an entirely different issue to be marrying someone she didn't like! Goodness, that was a revelation!

She looked around, heard Evan's loud laughter followed by his friends' and she thought about a lifetime of this. Was this what she really wanted?

Sierra stepped away from her friends and grabbed her coat. Slipping out of the house, she moved around to the side yard where she wouldn't be seen through the windows of the house as easily. She was a bit stunned by her latest revelation and needed a moment to…well, to be relieved! She could breathe more easily all of a sudden and she lifted her head up to the moon, relishing the cool air on her cheeks.

It was cold out here, with snow still on the ground. But the fresh air felt better than the stuffiness inside. She hadn't realized how stifled she felt until she could breathe in the fresh air. Stifled by Evan, her mother and father's expectations for her life and an engagement that made absolutely no sense.

This was a mistake, she thought. She couldn't marry Evan. She didn't love him. Good grief, she didn't even like him!

"Aren't you supposed to be inside being the life of the party?"

Sierra spun around, startled by the deep voice. All she could see was a hand moving in the shadows as the man in question lifted his drink to his lips. But she knew who he was! That man's presence was too intense for her to mistake him for anyone else.

"Goodness, you startled me, Your Grace," she said and pulled her wool coat closer around her body. She felt good, she thought. Really good! She'd break off her engagement to Evan tomorrow and she'd be free! Free to figure out what she really wanted for her life.

Even in the darkness, this man's image popped into her head. But she shook that thought away. This man wasn't what she wanted for her future, she told herself firmly. This man was out of her league. He was tall, dark and terrifying and definitely not for her. But he was gorgeous, she thought. That was a safe thing to contemplate since it was undeniable.

Harrison watched the woman and thought there was something different about her. A vitality that had been missing when he'd first been introduced to her. And damn, but that excited look about her eyes only made her more attractive. He'd come outside to get away from her, away from the confused expression in her eyes as he'd watched her over the past hour. He'd wanted to smash her fiancée's face in. Not for any good reason other than pure, unadulterated jealousy. Harrison was jealous that the idiotic man got to touch this gentle beauty, to kiss her and have a future with him.

That in itself was startling because he hadn't wanted a future with any woman. There were too many of them out there that he could enjoy, why settle for one? Of course, there was that ridiculous caveat of his inheritance, but he quickly dismissed that. He refused to rely upon his inheritance for anything. He'd made his own way in the world and his empire now made his inheritance seem like a pittance. Let the title pass on to someone else, he thought. The rules surrounding the damn title were ridiculous and outdated. He refused to be tied to antiquated rules that he didn't agree with and wouldn't comply with either.

Staring at this woman in the moonlight, a sparkle to her gaze that made his body harden with excitement, he thought about her rosebud lips and her soft, pale skin. She was beautiful, he thought and his body reacted even more, making him grateful for his coat that could hide his body's reaction. "I apologize," he said and stepped out of the shadows. "Just having a bit of quiet myself."

She smiled, pulling her coat closer around her shoulders. "I'll leave you to your drink," she said.

"Please don't," he said just as she was turning to go back inside. "Stay and talk to me. I have business with your father but I know nothing about you."

That was a startling statement and she spoke before she even realized what she was going to say. "There's no need to know about me," she said, her voice soft in the night.

He didn't respond for a long moment, his eyes taking in the pink of her cheeks, visible because of the light from the full moon. "I think there's every need," he finally replied.

Sierra's smile widened and she felt her heart race. That never happened when she was around Evan. Or any of the men she'd casually dated in the past. Her heart rate had always remained calm and unruffled. Not with this man though!

"There isn't really anything to tell." She wished that were different. And it might be different in the future, now that she'd woken up, figuratively speaking.

"How did you meet your fiancée?" he asked.

Sierra looked out at the dormant gardens, feeling like they represented her life. "My father suggested we go out," she explained. And even that explanation bothered her now that she realized it. "I don't remember why," she went on and she heard the puzzled quality in her voice.

Instinctively, she looked up into the man's eyes even though she couldn't really see them in the darkness. "I guess it just sort of…happened."

He moved closer to her and Sierra's heart pounded harder with each of his steps. "Do you normally let life just sweep you along in its path?"

She thought about that and didn't like the answer that popped into her mind. "I think I do, actually." She blinked back the tears of shame with that admission. "I didn't realize it until tonight."

Harrison wanted her smile back. He was disturbed by her tears and had a strange, unprecedented need to take her into his arms, to comfort her somehow. "What made you come to that startling realization?"

She laughed self-consciously. "I guess my eyes woke up at his behavior tonight around his friends." She stepped back and looked out again at the snow covered garden. "He's not a gentleman," she announced.

Harrison chuckled at her startled discovery but he had to agree with her. Evan Winters was an ass. "Not many men are. We're pretty much trained to conquer and destroy." He moved behind her, looking down at the top of her head.

She could feel the heat emanating from him and she wanted to curl up against him, to feel those strong arms around her. But she closed her own arms over her stomach instead. "Is that a warning?" she asked, trying for a teasing tone.

He was startled by her question, but had to admit that he enjoyed her quick mind. She wasn't just a beautiful face, he thought. But he also suspected that she didn't know that herself. "Are you saying that I would be able to conquer you, Sierra?" he asked softly.

Sierra turned around, her eyes blinking up to his. "Would you want to?" she whispered, every muscle in her body frozen as she waited for his response.

"Oh yes," he replied without hesitation.

Without waiting for permission, he leaned his head down and kissed her. His kiss wasn't gentle or tentative as she was used to. As promised, he conquered her. Even his hands moved up, cupping the back of her head and pulling her head back so that his tongue could invade her mouth.

Sierra shivered, thrilled by his dominance. She lifted up onto her toes, trying to get closer to him, to feel him against her. Unfortunately, her heavy coat obstructed her efforts. She wasn't aware of the sounds of frustration she was making until she felt his hands pushing the wool out of the way, his hands moving against her.

The sensations washing over her were all new and she wasn't sure how to handle them. But when she felt his hand slide up her waist to cup her breast, she gasped in surprise and horror as the reality of what she was doing broke through the sensual haze that had surrounded the two of them.

She pulled back, her startled eyes looking up at him.

Harrison pulled back reluctantly. He was stunned by what he'd just done. Kissing an engaged woman really wasn't his style.

"I guess that's how men conquer and destroy," he teased.

Sierra's fingers moved up to her lips, so horrified by her actions that she took his words in the worst possible way. Lashing out, she stepped backwards, her hands, in fact, her whole body shaking in reaction to both his kiss and the very strange way he had made her feel as well as her undignified actions. She was ashamed!

"I deserved that. And I guess that shows me exactly how you view me." She turned away. "I suppose I should have listened to your warning more thoroughly. I thought you were different from Evan, more dignified and gentlemanly. But you're not," she snapped. "You're just like him, although a panther in a better suit!" With those parting words, she spun around and walked away, pulling her coat closer around her as she hurried to find a place to lick her wounds.

"Sierra…" he started to tell her that he hadn't thought that at all. But her hand came up, stopping his words.

"Please. You're right. That was promiscuous of me. And you didn't deserve my censure. All of my censure should rest solely on my shoulders." She bowed her head even as she stepped away from him. "Please, forgive me."

Sierra hurried away, ashamed of her behavior and furious with him as well.

She heard him call out to her but quickened her steps, needing to get away from the disturbing man.

Most of her disgust was centered on herself. She'd just decided to break off her engagement to one man and started kissing another? How could she have been so immoral? To let a stranger kiss her, and at her engagement party no less! Her only excuse was that she'd felt so free and he was a fascinating man. Not a good excuse. It still made her feel cheap and tawdry.

She'd have to break up with Evan, she thought as she slipped upstairs to the privacy of her bedroom. She berated herself for her actions and, when she was able to calm down, she knew that she thoroughly deserved the stranger's words. She'd been wanton and there was no reason he should think she was anything better than a whore. Her actions proved that. She was kissing a stranger at her engagement party!

That realization kept lashing at her and she sank down lower onto her bed, trying to ease her shame but nothing could lessen the crazy feelings that were bouncing around inside of her. Evan had never kissed her like that, nor had she ever felt anything when he touched her. Possibly revulsion, she thought with regret and Sierra layered more disgust on her shoulders because she hadn't realized what she was feeling, had simply let life carry her forward without making any real decisions herself.

She sat in the darkness of her bedroom, her wool coat still wrapped around her as she listened absently to the sounds of the party below. How soon could she break off her engagement to Evan? She had to do it quickly but would that man actually brag about kissing her? She wouldn't put anything past the stranger. Or any man, for that matter!

Maybe she should be grateful to the man. Maybe he'd done her a favor by reinforcing her decision to stop her engagement. Before that stupid kiss, she'd come to the realization that she'd just been floating through life, not really directing her existence. And she didn't love Evan. Not even a little bit.

That thought only increased her self-flagellations and she wanted to bury her head underneath her pillow in shame, but she forced herself to face some ugly truths. She was aimless. She had no idea what she wanted to do with her life and she was simply coasting along, letting others direct her.

That had to stop. She had to regain, or gain control since she'd never really taken control, and figure out what she wanted for her life.

Happiness, she thought instantly.

But how did one go about finding that elusive emotion? An image of the tall, dark-eyed man floated through her mind but she banished his image. He was the wrong man for her, for so many reasons.

First thing tomorrow, she was taking control, she thought with renewed determination.

Pushing herself off of the floor, she got ready for bed, uncaring that her engagement party was still going strong one floor beneath her. It was more for Evan to mingle with clients than it was a celebration of their engagement. The engagement had only been the excuse. If he hadn't proposed, her father and Patrick would have come up with another reason to throw a party for their clients. They always found a reason.

Unfortunately, she never got the chance to grab hold of that control. The doorbell rang early the next morning and, before anyone could understand what was happening, her father was being dragged away in handcuffs. Apparently, he'd been embezzling money from several of his clients' accounts, including the Duke of Selton's, which put him in real danger.

While the family was still reeling from that horror, a week later, Sierra's mother took an overdose of sleeping pills. Her humiliation among all of her friends over her husband's arrest was too much for her, apparently. Since her whole identity was wrapped up in her role as a wife and a society hostess, she couldn't live when that was taken away from her.

Sierra stood by her mother's graveside next to her brother without any other mourners as the freezing rain slowly soaked through their winter coats, she wondered why her mother had taken the easy route. She refused to cry as her mother's body was lowered into the ground, her anger over her mother's suicide creating so many conflicting emotions within her that she simply wasn't sure what to feel. Her father wasn't allowed to attend the funeral because he was considered a flight risk, so it was just Sierra and Daniel standing by their mother's grave, confused and lost with mounting debt as the legal fees to defend their father started mounting up and the family's bank accounts were frozen.

She'd cried so much over that week but she was soon to find out that her life was not finished catapulting out of control.

Her father was not well, he claimed to be innocent but, with all of his money frozen, Sierra had no idea how to pay for a solicitor to defend her father. This was all outside of her experience but she was going to figure it out! She had to! This was her family, as dysfunctional as they might be, and she had to deal with it. Her mother had taken the easy way out. Sierra wasn't going to do that, not to Daniel or to her father.

Adding to everything else, Evan arrived at the house right after her mother's funeral. Pushing through the front door, he berated Sierra for her father's crimes. He was furious with her for humiliating him like this and Sierra was too numb to defend herself. She hadn't even taken off her coat, the heavy wool weighing her down just as Evan's accusations were doing.

She couldn't seem to form the words to explain that she hadn't done anything to him, that it was her father who had been arrested and even then, she didn't believe her father capable of what the accusations. Evan's words were harsh and his attitude brutal as he dismissed her from his life, demanding the diamond engagement ring back as if he were some sort of king that had to retract his presence from a menial subject.

As she slid the gaudy ring off of her finger, she felt a small bit of relief. She hadn't realized how much her engagement to Evan was weighing on her mind. She'd meant to break it off with him several days ago but circumstances and timing were never right.

The final pain came when an officer showed up at her door the day after her mother's funeral, informing her that her father had suffered a massive heart attack and died overnight in his jail cell.

As she stared at the officer, her hand cold on the freezing doorknob, she almost laughed at the insanity that her life had become.

But she couldn't laugh. She couldn't cry. In seven days, her world had been destroyed. Her father had been arrested, her mother had committed suicide, her fiancée had broken off their engagement and now this. Her life as she'd known it was over. She couldn't even react to the officer's words, just stared at him through the open doorway while the man awkwardly tried to come up with some words to express his sympathy. But the sympathy wasn't there and the officer just floundered. Sierra wasn't sure what she was feeling now. Her father was gone? That must not be right. Her mother had been buried only yesterday. It had been raining. Evan had…

Her only response was to close the door and walk into the living room where, a week earlier, her father's friends, business associates and clients had mingled, celebrating her upcoming marriage. Everything had changed. Everything was…

She wasn't sure how to describe her life now. Daniel burst into the room, furious and with another bloody nose but Sierra had no idea how to react. Thankfully, he rushed up to his room, relieving her of the need to form any response. He was understandably angry and confused because his life had been thrown into chaos as well. He was closer to their mother but he was also missing their father as well. Not to mention, he had to go to school and be around the other kids, all of whom were cruel and abusive, thinking that Daniel's father had been a thief. So not only had he lost his parents, but he'd lost his entire network of friends, practically overnight.

She'd thought that things couldn't get any worse. Unfortunately, fate was not finished torturing her. A solicitor arrived on her doorstep the following week, informing her that her house was being taken over by her father's investment firm. It would be sold, including all of the contents, in order to pay back the investors.

Sierra heard the words but she couldn't figure out what they meant. She'd lost her mother, her father, her fiancée and now she was about to lose her home?

The solicitor finally left, leaving the eviction papers on the coffee table while she stared into space. This wasn't happening, she told herself as the cold seeped into her body. It simply could not be happening. She had lost so much and now she was going to lose the only home she'd ever known?

Sierra had no idea how long she'd sat there but by the time she stood, her legs ached and it was dark. She hadn't eaten anything in...well, she couldn't remember the last time she'd eaten. She looked at the contents of the pantry but closed the door, unable to stomach any food.

Just over two weeks ago, she'd come alive. She'd woken up. She'd realized that her life was being directed by someone else.

Oh, how silly she'd been.

Now her life was completely out of control!

Chapter 1

Present day…

Sierra glanced at her watch with rising frustration and worry. As usual, Daniel was late. At nineteen, he should be going off to university but instead, he was hanging out with the wrong crowd, ignoring the need to help put food on the table or pay the rent and still acting like a spoiled brat. She wasn't sure what to do about him but she was becoming increasingly anxious about his activities. She loved him and knew that he had been struggling with all that had occurred during his teen years. It had been a hard period after her father's arrest. But they'd gotten through it.

She had a job, they had a small cottage that they rented and, if her best friends were still the horses she used to ride, that was perfectly fine with her. She had classes too! She was studying to become a veterinarian, something that had occurred to her about a year after her father's funeral. She'd been working in the stables, the same stables that her father had owned, and one of the horses had gotten sick. She'd known exactly what was wrong and how to treat the animal, and when the vet showed up, he'd encouraged her to think about joining the profession. He'd said she had an instinct for animals that would help her in the industry.

So she'd thought about it. And the more she'd considered the idea, the more it appealed to her. She absolutely loved the thought of helping animals, taking care of them. So she'd signed up and had been taking one or two classes each semester, thoroughly enjoying the intellectual stimulation of the program.

No longer was she simply floating along in life. Nope, she had goals, she had ambition. And it felt good. For the first time in a long time, she felt alive. At the end of the day, she could honestly say that she was happy.

It would be nice if she could banish a man's kiss from her dreams, but if that was the only lasting repercussion from the mess in her life back then, she could deal with it. Perhaps it would be easier to get the tall, arrogant duke out of her mind if she didn't work for him. After their eviction, he'd bought her family's house and the stables along with all of the horses. The only job she could find after her father's arrest was in the stables. And she was thrilled for the work, not embarrassed at all to be working in a place her family previously owned. Of course, Daniel hated that fact. He also teased her unmercifully when the owner came to visit because Sierra hid from him, unable to face him. Daniel had no idea why she hid every time the Duke of Selton came for a weekend. There was no way she'd ever tell anyone about the fire she'd felt every time he tried to talk to her, the heat just at the memory of that kiss…or the humiliation.

She pushed the Duke of Selton out of her mind. He was simply her employer. A very handsome, very devastatingly charming employer…but that was it. She couldn't think of him in any other terms. She was happy with her life, she was directing her world and doing something she loved. Thinking about that kiss was counter-productive.

So what if she didn't date anyone? She might be comparing every man she met against the Duke of Selton's shockingly large, amazingly muscular physique. But maybe that was just self-protection. Maybe she just didn't want to get involved with any other man.

Sierra sighed as she pondered the man, her brother, her future, her world. Things were going well, she thought with pride. Her world had been destroyed but she'd picked up the pieces and moved forward. She had to push that particular man out of her mind and focus on the things that counted in life.

If only she could somehow curb her brother's antics now. Daniel was going to severely hurt his future if he didn't stop hanging out with those boys on the corner. Why couldn't he see that a job and an education were his ticket out of his resentment and anger over the hand fate had dealt him? Yes, their life had been destroyed when her father's embezzlement had been discovered. No, it wasn't fair! Nothing about their predicament back then had been fair. But that was no excuse to simply be angry for the rest of one's life. He needed to fight back, to regain control and get an education, prove everyone wrong when they whispered that he was a bad apple.

Unfortunately, every time she tried to tell him this, he would either laugh at her encouragement or scoff at her menial job. "You muck out stalls, Sierra!" he'd shouted at her one day. "How is that dignified?"

He was right though. She did muck out the stalls. And cleaned the stables, brushed down the horses, hauled hay and oats…the list of her chores each day was exhausting. But she loved it. And she was getting paid to do a good day's work not to mention learning more about animals and what they needed to stay healthy. That was something that her parents had never encouraged her to do.

Looking back, she realized that her parent's only goal for her was to marry well and follow in her mother's footsteps. But her mother had been miserable. Sierra had known that her mother had slipped bourbon into her coffee every afternoon. And she'd been taking sleeping pills for years. There had probably been other drugs as well but Sierra hadn't known what was really going on. Everything had been a façade of happiness and a falsely glorious future. Her mother had lived for her father's success and looking good to her "friends", all of whom had immediately abandoned her after her husband's arrest. Not real friends, Sierra had thought on more than one occasion.

It had been brutal when she'd lost both of her parents within one week. The humiliation of having her father arrested hadn't been a cakewalk either. But now she knew that it had been a wakeup call. No, none of it was fair. And it was tragic on too many levels to count. Dwelling on that though would destroy her mentally. It had happened. It wasn't good or right or fair, but it was what happened. Moving forward was the only answer. Dwelling on the past and letting the anger fester was not the right answer. She stirred the contents of the stew and wondered how she could help Daniel see it the same way. He was just so angry!

She breathed a bit easier when she heard noises outside the cottage indicating that he had finally arrived home.

"Hi there!" she greeted him as he clambered through the door. He was more exuberant than normal and she felt the muscles in her shoulders relax. When the boy was angry, he was a beast to be around.

"Hi there!" he replied, dumping his backpack onto the rough, kitchen table she'd found in a thrift store. "Guess what?"

She looked over her shoulder, surprised to find him not just smiling, but beaming! "What?" she asked, turning around to give him her full attention.

"Our money problems are over!" he announced.

Sierra laughed. Their former home was owned by a man that confused completely, she was still mucking out stalls and, as far as she was aware, he still didn't have a job. "Okay, what's happened? Did you win the lottery?"

"Even better," he came right back. "We'd have to pay taxes on the lottery. This income is tax free!"

Sierra didn't like the sound of that. Her shoulders tensed up and her stomach felt ill all of a sudden. "Daniel, what have you done?" she demanded as she clutched the back of the wooden chair. Not a good support though because the chair was liable to break at the least provocation.

He shook his head. "You always go into hiding when your duke shows up at our house. And everything inside that house is our stuff anyway."

Her stomach tightened with her brother's words. The Duke of Selton wasn't "her" duke although she'd relived that damnable kiss too many times over the past three years. And every time, her body became hot and bothered, making her cringe with the feelings that still seemed so raw and intense. No matter how much she tried to rationalize her behavior, it still came down to the fact that she'd kissed a man while her fiancée was inside celebrating their engagement. And then there were his words. She didn't want to be conquered. Especially not by a man like him. He had been too tall, too sure of himself. And she didn't like tall men. She liked men who were kind and gentle. There had been nothing kind about that kiss.

It had been overpowering, overwhelming and completely domineering. She wanted a man who respected her, who would gently, kindly kiss her and love her in a generous fashion with words of love and expressions of affection.

She shook her head, pushing memories of that kiss out of her mind. Again. Too many times over the past three years she'd let herself relive that kiss. It was pointless, she thought. The man now owned her old home and came out to ride. During those times, she worked hard to be gone, out of sight. She never wanted to see that man again, too humiliated by her actions.

"What happened today?" she asked warily.

"I took it back!" he exclaimed.

She tensed even more. "What did you take back?" she demanded. As she stared at Daniel's excited expression, dread filled up her mind, causing her stomach to twist with dread. "What have you done?"

Daniel was oblivious to his older sister's worry. His smile broadened and his shoulders pulled back with pride as he explained, "I snuck into our house and stole some items. Some things that I know are valuable." And with that, he upended his backpack and dumped out the contents. There were the antique, gold frames that her mother had treasured more than anything, as well as several other knickknacks that Sierra knew were very valuable.

As she looked down at the items, she felt sick to her stomach. "What have you done?" she whispered.

Daniel was practically preening. "I've ensured that you can quit that disgusting job and go to school full time, Sierra. This is what we've needed all along. I can't believe I didn't think of this before. But when Will mentioned it…"

Her eyes flew from the stolen items on their beaten up table to his eagerly excited eyes. "Will Honfleur put you up to this?" she demanded, trying not to shout. "How many times have I told you that Will is nothing but trouble?!"

Daniel's eyebrows came down with irritation at her tone. "He's a good guy, Sierra. You should get to know him a bit before you judge him like that. He's not as bad as you might think."

She stared up at her brother who had grown about a foot since their parents' funeral. He now towered over Sierra and, because of his height, thought he should be free to do whatever he wanted. "How can you even suggest that he's not so bad when he suggested that you steal? And not just steal, but obviously, you broke into the man's house! That's breaking and entering! And it is a felony!" Sierra was dumbfounded that her brother had lowered himself to this level! It was impossible, wasn't it? Daniel was a good kid, he wasn't a thief!

But Daniel was furious that his efforts were now being spurned. He'd thought it was such a brilliant idea. Why was his sister so furious? "Sierra, that house and all of that land had been in our family for generations! Dad was a wealthy man! There's no way he would have stolen that money and you know it. So what happened to him was wrong!"

She'd heard this over and over again. For three years, she'd listened to Daniel spout those words. And she agreed with him but because her father died in jail, the investigation stopped. Everyone simply assumed his guilt, then she and Daniel had lost their house before they understood what was happening.

"So prove it!" she snapped back at him, furious that he'd put them both into a precarious position by stealing. "Prove it through legitimate channels. Don't go breaking the law and proving everyone right about our family!" She couldn't believe he didn't see what he was doing! All of their old friends had shunned them after their father's arrest. They'd thought the Warner family was tainted, that they were all from bad blood because of her father's supposed crimes. Now her brother goes out and proves all of their assumptions correct by stealing? She simply couldn't figure him out sometimes!

Daniel disagreed. "No one will even know that this stuff is gone, Sierra," he told her with a voice that tried to tease her out of her anger. "I took those back stairs through the basement, the ones that no one probably knows about. And besides, we lived in that house since we were born. I know how to get through all of the rooms without setting off the motion detectors and I know where all of the alarms are. So your duke will never know that we took anything."

She shoved her fingers into her hair, trying to figure out what to do now, how to convince him that his heist was going to ruin everything for them, and most likely get him arrested. Her baby brother had broken into a man's house and stolen property! This was horrible! And if she didn't turn him in, she would be an accomplice to the crime! With all of that, she focused on the one thing he'd said that she could tackle. All the rest was just…it was too much to comprehend! "Would you please stop calling him that? He's not 'my' anything!"

Daniel smirked, crossing his arms over his lanky chest and looking down at his sister. "Then why were you all googly eyed when the man walked into the party three years ago? And why were you kissing him out on the patio?"

She gasped and stared up at him. "I wasn't…" How could Daniel have seen that kiss? She'd been over to the side, out of the way of the windows. Not that she'd been trying to hide. That kiss had been…well, it had taken both of them by surprise. At least, she hoped that the Duke of Selton hadn't planned that interlude. Or had he? No, that was crazy, she thought. Besides, he'd already been outside. There was no way he could have known she was coming out for a breath of fresh air. Even she hadn't known she was going to do that.

"I saw you, Sierra," he told her with belligerence. "I was out by the stables with my friends."

She pushed her sandy-blond hair back out of her eyes, the shame washing over her once again. "Did anyone else see that?" she asked, bowing her head.

Daniel could tell that he'd really hurt her this time. He'd kept his mouth shut for years about what he'd seen, but when she was trying to tell him that he'd done something wrong when he'd finally found a way to make things right, he just couldn't hold back. "No, I was out smoking a cigarette. I was alone. The others were too cold. They went into the stables to hang out."

She let out the breath she'd been holding and sank down onto the rickety chair that she'd collected when someone had put it out for the trash. "It isn't that simple," she told him as she rubbed her temples. "If there is one thing I've learned over the past three, nightmarish years, it is that nothing is ever that simple."

Daniel looked down at his sister, realizing that she was truly upset. "Are you okay, Sierra?" he asked softly. He didn't understand why a kiss had made her this distraught, but then again, he didn't really understand women anyway.

Sierra looked up at him, fighting back the tears. Every time she thought she was getting ahead of things, something happened to slap her back down. Daniel going on a crime spree was just the most current slap. She had a scary suspicion that, after today, she was going to long for the days when he would just get a speeding ticket or arrested for loitering. The penalties for those kinds of offenses were just a slap on the wrist.

Breaking and entering, not to mention grand larceny, was on a whole new level.

"Take the stuff back, Daniel," she pleaded with him. "Just bring it back before the man even knows that it is gone."

Chapter 2

"What's wrong?" Scarlett asked as she floated into Harrison's office. "You look like someone just stole your favorite tie." She laughed at that since Harrison didn't have a favorite anything. He worked hard to hide his softer side to the world and liking something too much would make him vulnerable. The man detested weakness in any form.

Harrison glanced across his desk as the blond woman stood waiting for a retort. Instead of replying, he spun his laptop around.

"What's that?" she asked, stepping forward slightly.

Harrison just pressed the play button again, letting her watch and discover for herself.

Scarlett saw the blank look on his handsome features and knew something was very, very wrong. The more bored or blank Harrison looked, the worse things were. That old British stoicism kicked in at times like this.

She wasn't sure what she was looking at but saw only a darkened room. She recognized the furniture though. "Isn't that…" she stopped speaking when she saw movement. A kid, a teen actually, was moving around the darkened area, slipping things into a backpack. "Is he…?"

"Yes," Harrison hissed furiously. He stood up impatiently and walked to the window, looking out over the Thames River. But he didn't see the churning water or the sunshine, the tourists that were eagerly heading over the bridge or taking pictures of Parliament. All he saw was the glowing, confused eyes of a woman on the brink of making a major discovery about herself. Even after three years, he still remembered those soft, grey eyes and the brilliance, followed by that kiss. That extraordinary kiss. Damn, his body still reacted to that damn kiss.

He almost cursed when his body hardened with need. Just like it had three years ago. Just like it did every time he went by that house to try and see her.

"Harrison, isn't that the brother of that girl…" Once again, Scarlett didn't have to finish the sentence.

The door opened again and another man walked into Harrison's office. "What did I miss?" Stefan Kozlov asked, looking at the two other occupants. The Russian man instantly knew something was wrong. "Damon?"

Scarlett shook her head, understanding the unspoken question. "No, he's fine. He took Sasha on another honeymoon. We haven't heard anything from him."

"That's a good thing," Malik interrupted as he walked into Harrison's office next. "Why is everyone looking glum?" Malik looked down at Scarlett. "Where's Grayson?"

Scarlett's eyes flashed. "I have no idea. Why do you guys always ask me where Grayson is? It isn't like I'm his keeper," she said and pulled her gloves out of her purse, trying to appear unconcerned regarding the whereabouts of the last member of their group.

The three others looked at each other, suppressing their amusement at her attempt to hide her feelings for the other member of their motley assemblage. But they all knew her too well and could see the signs.

"Sorry, love," Malik replied, bending down and kissing her head. "Just asking a question. No need to ruffle your lovely feathers."

Harrison cleared his throat and looked behind Malik significantly. Malik turned around and almost burst out laughing at the furious expression in Grayson's eyes. If the man didn't do something about his feelings for Scarlett, the others were going to have to take some action. The woman couldn't wait forever!

Scarlett turned around, already sensing that the American had entered the office. "You're late," she snapped, hiding her excitement at seeing the tall, dark haired man behind an irritated façade.

Grayson's sharp brown eyes flicked in her direction, then quickly away. "And you're prissy," he came right back but he moved over to kiss her as well. "Don't be prissy."

Scarlett's eyes flashed and the other men suspected she wanted to punch the American who knew how to press her buttons better than anyone. "I'll be as prissy as I want," she came right back. "But I'll bet I could take you down."

He chuckled, taking her arm and leading her out of the office. "I'd like to see that happen."

The others watched as Scarlett, the only woman in their group, the only woman who had ever been allowed in their private lunches simply because she refused to allow herself to be excluded, walked beside Grayson, closer than was necessary for a woman who professed not to be madly in love with the man. They all knew that was a lie. And they all knew that Grayson Brooks was just as passionately in love with Scarlett. The two of them just had bad timing. Every time Grayson was in between mistresses, Scarlett found a lap dog of a man to escort her around. When Scarlett finally came to her senses, Grayson had gone out and chosen another mistress.

There had been talk of an intervention between the others but so far, it was just too amusing to watch the two of them snap at each other one moment, then get as close as possible to each other the next. Just like now, Scarlett stood next to Grayson, her arm almost, but not quite touching Grayson's arm. Harrison, Stefan and Malik stood on the opposite side of the elevator, the three of them watching to see what would happen between Scarlett and Grayson.

"When Damon comes back?" Harrison finally suggested, breaking the silence when Scarlett and Grayson stood stiffly still beside each other.

Stefan and Malik both nodded their heads, instantly understanding. Scarlett and Grayson both looked over at them, their eyes questioning. "What happens when Damon comes back?" Grayson asked.

Harrison shook his head, indicating that it wasn't very important. It was actually. Vitally important. But it wasn't a message intended for either Scarlett or Grayson.

"What are you going to do about the boy?" Scarlett asked as they all entered the elevator together.

Harrison sighed. "I can't let him get away with it."

Malik, Stefan and Grayson looked at Harrison, not sure what they were talking about.

Scarlett filled them in. "Do you remember three years ago when that guy embezzled millions from Harrison?" On the way to the restaurant, she filled them in on what she'd seen on the computer.

The three men nodded their heads, their body language shifting slightly into attack mode. She saw the subtle change and ignored it. This group of men defended one another like no other friends she'd ever seen. It hadn't always been like that. The first day she'd met the five of them, they'd been at each other's throats. Literally. Her uncle, the headmaster at the boarding school they'd all attended, had been at his wits end, trying to get them to stop fighting. It wasn't until she'd arrived that the boys all figured out they were better together than fighting one another. And God help the rest of the world now! When one was in trouble, the others were ready to attack. They were a formidable force within the global business community.

Every once in a while, someone came along and was stupid enough to try and compete with one or all of them. One of these men alone was terrifying and could easily handle any threat. But put all of them together? And they were a force to be reckoned with.

As often as possible, these men adjusted their schedule to meet. Sometimes it was for a lunch, like today, and other times, they were all able to carve out a weekend, meeting up at one house or another or find a resort that could occupy them for the long weekend. They now lived all over the world, but they made this friendship a priority. Even Malik, who ran a powerful, wealthy country, took time to meet for lunches like this. The security measures involved were monumental since each one of them was disgustingly wealthy on their own. Put them all together and their security teams worked better than the Secret Service protecting the US President.

They'd reached the restaurant and, over lunch, Harrison filled them in on the theft as well as what he knew about the brother and sister, keeping his own fascination with the daughter to himself. No need for this group to hear about that debacle, he thought.

"So what are you going to do about the boy?" Grayson asked when coffee was served.

Harrison shook his head, shifting his coffee cup on the saucer slightly. "I have no idea."

Malik rubbed his chin. "The woman, is she still around?" he asked, remembering a long ago conversation when Harrison had explained the embezzlement, mentioning a blond haired "beauty".

Stefan smiled slightly. "She works in his stables. Didn't he mention that?"

Harrison glared at Stefan. "She needed a job. She didn't embezzle the money. She'd lost her parents, her fiancée and her house all in the span of two weeks. And no one would give her a job."

Grayson's eyebrows went up. "She works for you? In your stables?"

Harrison stared down at the black coffee. "She's been working there since about two months after she was evicted from her home."

Scarlett's eyes widened. "How did you know that she hadn't been able to get a job?"

Harrison stared at her from across the table. "I knew," was all he would say.

And to all the others at the table, they understood what had not been spoken. Scarlett smothered her excitement that perhaps Harrison might have found his "one and only". "So you're going to rescue the boy?" She leaned forward, her romantic heart started beating and it had nothing to do with the fact that Grayson had put his arm onto the back of her chair. Nothing at all!

But then she remembered that Harrison had a deadline. He didn't have time to mess around with a woman who might not want him back. "Actually, you don't have time for this. You know that the deadline is looming. And my offer still stands."

Harrison winked at the woman but shook his head. "I appreciate the offer but no. That would definitely not work out well."

Grayson sat up straighter, sensing that the two of them had discussed an option out of Harrison's predicament that was completely unacceptable. "What offer did you propose?" he asked. Everyone knew what deadline was looming. And anything that had to do with Scarlett, he wanted to know about.

Stefan put a hand on Grayson's shoulder as he said, "He turned down her offer."

Grayson still glared at Harrison. "What the hell is going on?"

Scarlett put a hand on his other arm and, instantly, he relaxed. "I offered to help him, Grayson. It is the same thing each of you would do under similar circumstances if you had the power to help him. But none of you have that ability. I do."

Grayson stared into her soft, blue eyes and his gut tightened as he realized what she'd offered. He turned his head, his eyes lasering into Harrison's.

Harrison lifted his hands, palms up. "I turned her down, mate," he said with a chuckle.

"But if things get too close," Scarlett spoke up but didn't finish the sentence.

"You're cutting it pretty close already," Malik commented. His eyes were looking carefully at his friend. "Is there a reason why you have not chosen someone?"

Harrison shifted in his seat. "I'll take care of it," he told the group. "Don't worry." And already his mind was spinning, an idea forming. "In fact, I have a pretty good idea of how things will get fixed." He rubbed the edge of his coffee cup with his forefinger, the idea forming in his mind, making more sense than anything had in a long time. "In fact, I suspect that I can wrap this issue up quite quickly."

Scarlett watched his handsome features and a chill went down her spine. All of these men were so dangerously powerful, when they set out to implement a plan, she wouldn't like to be the one in the crosshairs.

Chapter 3

Harrison pulled up outside the tiny cottage, looking at the chipped paint on the wooden shutters and the tiny flowers that were struggling to survive. Sierra had planted those, he observed. And just like the woman, they were not thriving. The spring had started off warmer than average, lulling everyone into a belief that winter had finally gone away. But then a cold snap had arrived and brought everyone back to the awareness that Mother Nature liked to taunt.

Lifting his computer, he stepped out of the limousine. He'd been given the woman's schedule so he knew that she was home. And since he hadn't called his housekeeper to give her a head's up of his arrival, there was no way that the lovely Sierra Warner could escape him this time. He knew that she disappeared every time he came to the house and yes, it irritated him.

But now his skittish little colt was unable to bolt. And he was about to close the trap even further.

Sierra wiped her hands on the threadbare dishtowel, her stomach tightening in dread when she heard the car rolling down the gravel driveway, coming to a stop in front of her small cottage. Daniel hadn't been home in several days. Initially, she'd thought he was only staying with friends but no one had seen him in a while. Now someone was at her door and she just knew that it wasn't going to be good. The few friends she had in the village wouldn't ring the doorbell. They would simply knock and walk into the cottage. Formality wasn't ever observed and Sierra had loved that part of her life.

So now she stood in the tiny kitchen, staring at the wooden front door, praying that this wasn't more bad news. Praying that it wasn't an officer arriving to tell her that Daniel had been arrested for breaking and entering, theft or some other horrific charge. The only reason someone would ring the doorbell, in her experience lately, was to bring bad news.

She considered not answering it. She stared at the door, thinking that it would be nice to just walk into her tiny bedroom and pull the covers up over her head. She wanted to hide from the world, ignore all of the bad things that were looming just on the other side of that door.

But that was a coward's way out. And she refused to be a coward. Her mother had taken that route and Sierra would be stronger. She would not bow down to the world that continuously threatened to smother her. Eventually, the bad news would have to end. There was only so much bad that a person could take before something good happened. The tide of bad luck had to change eventually!

When she opened the door and saw the tall, shockingly handsome man on the other side, she conceded that today was not the day in which that tide would turn.

"What are you doing here?" she demanded, wishing she had taken a few moments to brush her hair. Or put on a bit of makeup. The man standing in her doorway looked…amazing! His cashmere coat appeared warm and soft while everything about the man himself seemed hard and uncompromising.

"We need to talk," he told her with a firm tone. "May I come in?"

Sierra noticed the hard look in those navy blue eyes, a look that made her stomach muscles tighten even further. She shook her head. "No. I don't think so."

He raised one dark eyebrow. "I really don't think you want this to go further than the two of us, Sierra." The message was clear; let him in or deal with the authorities.

Sierra bristled with his tone. "The last time I saw you, my world fell apart afterwards. I'm not willing to make that mistake again." Despite the fact that her brother had stolen priceless antiques from this man's house, she still couldn't be polite to him! No, she couldn't let him in. He was dangerous in so many ways!

Harrison refrained from chuckling at her comment. Even when he knew she was terrified, she was still saucy and adorable. "I don't believe I was the catalyst for the unfortunate events after our last encounter. Invite me inside, Sierra."

Her hands were knotting the dishtowel while her mind tried to figure out an escape plan. She wasn't sure if she wanted to throw herself into his arms and feel the excitement of that kiss, or slam the door in his face and accept that the police would be next. Either option was…shocking.

He saw the look in her eyes, anticipated what she was thinking and shook his head. "There's no way out of this."

Sierra stiffened with his words, irritated that he'd read her mind so accurately. He'd done that before and she hadn't liked it then. "Stop doing that!" she snapped. "And no, go away. I don't want to see you ever again," she told him and stepped backwards, about to close the door. It was a petty and, she knew, and an ineffectual, knee jerk reaction, but she was out of her depths with this man.

Harrison put a firm hand against the door, stopping her ability to shut him out. "I'll return, Sierra. And next time, the police will be with me."

The door froze and a moment later, she swung it wide. "You wouldn't!" she begged. But the look in his eyes told him that he would. Definitely, the bastard would do it! He would gleefully lead the police into the situation and she would once again be bogged down in a legal battle that she couldn't win.

"Come in!" she allowed and opened the door so that he could enter. He had to duck down because of his height and she took guilty pleasure in the fact that he had to continue ducking because of the beams on the cottage ceiling.

"Would you like some tea?" she offered, trying to be gracious but it was difficult. This man and all he knew about her, about that night, that kiss…he knew! Oh, goodness, she'd admitted things to him that night that she'd only realized moments before. And then he'd kissed her! She'd been celebrating her engagement to another man and…

What did he know now? Surely he could only suspect what Daniel had done, right? He couldn't have proof! If he had hard evidence, the man would go to the police, wouldn't he?

She tried to relax, thinking that if he knew anything definite, he wouldn't be here. The police would be at her door and Daniel would be in handcuffs.

Harrison watched as the lovely woman twisted a dishtowel around her red, chapped hands. He wished he could make everything right for this delicate beauty but today was not the day for that. But he could help her. She just had to accept his arrangement.

Thinking that giving her something to do might ease her tension, he nodded his head at her offer of tea. "That would be nice, thank you," he replied. He then sat down on the precarious chair and opened his laptop. "Do you know where your brother is?" he asked carefully, watching her lovely features to try and determine if she was telling the truth or not.

Sierra cringed at his words even while she filled up the tea kettle, setting it carefully on the burner to heat the water. "I haven't seen him in several days," she replied, trying to hide the worry. She was relieved that she could honestly reply to that question. Lying was extremely difficult for her.

But then something occurred to her and she swung around, looking at the enormous man who was sitting in the spindly chair, making it look even more unstable. "Is he okay? Have the…" she started to ask if the police had gotten him but then this man would know.

Harrison understood what she refused to ask. "No. The police don't have your brother. That's why I'm here," he explained. He pressed a few buttons on the keyboard. "You need to see this."

Sierra had just turned on the heat for the water under the teapot but she turned around, her eyes wide as she looked from his midnight blue eyes to the computer screen. "What's this?" she asked. Please, God, don't let this be that evidence she was so terrified of! Please let her finally have a break!

Harrison watched her carefully and saw the color drain out of her lovely features. "This is security footage of my house from a few days ago. My security team brought it to me the day after this happened."

Her eyes moved down to the screen and she felt the nausea well up inside of her as she recognized the living room of her old house. Before he even appeared on the screen, Sierra knew that the security cameras had captured her brother stealing those objects. Sure enough, seconds later, Daniel was caught walking blithely into the elegant living room as if he still owned the house. She watched with dread as he picked up several objects, put them into his backpack, all with a smug smile on his handsome features.

When the video ended, the teapot was whistling. But Sierra heard nothing other than the sound of her life falling apart once again. Daniel was going to be arrested and not even a good lawyer could help him. Not with this kind of evidence. He was going to prison, he'd be hurt and he'd lose his entire future, all because he'd done one stupid, imbecilic action! Her brother was just confused but underneath all of his anger, there was a sweet, funny kid just trying to figure out how to grow up.

Now he wouldn't! He'd be stuck in a cell and his whole life would be ruined!

She'd lose her job! And everyone around the village who had been starting to accept her, starting to talk to her once again, would be reminded that her father had been a criminal. They would know that her brother was also a criminal. All the stories, all the rumors, the lies and the truths, would be brought up once again, rehashed at the coffee shop and over tea in each person's cottage. It would be the same nightmare all over again!

"He's really a good kid," she whispered through numb lips. She watched as Harrison stood up and turned the heat off from the stove. He poured the water into both cups and brought one back to her. She wrapped her cold hands around the ceramic, painfully aware of his extremely large frame sitting back down across from her at the tiny table. "He's just…confused. And angry about what happened to him when my father was…" she couldn't say the words. It was too hard. But she couldn't let anything happen to Daniel! He was all she had left! He was her family and it was her job to protect him, even against himself if that was needed.

"Yes. I can imagine that was a great shock," Harrison said and sipped his tea. "But that doesn't excuse criminal behavior."

She lowered her head but didn't really see the cup in her hands. All she saw was her brother being carted away in handcuffs, just like what had happened to her father.

A hand rose up, her fingers pressing against her forehead as she contemplated what could happen. "Please, don't arrest him. I've told him to put the items back. Surely he's done that by now."

Harrison looked at the woman who was obviously in pain. Her only living relative had just committed a crime, which had additionally been caught on video. There was really no way that the boy could get out of this crime. He didn't want to do this, he thought. He wanted to pull her into his arms and command her to let him take care of this, to let him take care of her. He wanted to kiss her and hold her and make everything better for her.

But the stubborn tilt of her chin and the defiant way she was holding her shoulders told him that she wouldn't accept his help.

"I have a proposal," he offered. "We can help each other if you're willing."

Her eyes lifted again and he saw the sheen of tears she was fighting to keep under control. "A proposal?" she parroted, squaring her shoulders and refusing to look weak. She wasn't weak! She was strong and capable. She was pulling her life back together and this was not going to be the end! "What kind of a proposal?"

He leaned back and the triumphant look in his eyes made that horrible feeling in her stomach intensify. "I need an heir," he told her. "And I don't have a great deal of time to in order to produce that heir."

She opened and closed her mouth, confused and distrustful. Why would he tell her something like that? How could she help him? And what did this have to do with her brother potentially going to jail for a stupid, senseless crime? "What does that have to do with Daniel?" she asked, pressing her hands against the scarred, wooden table.

Harrison continued to watch her carefully. "That heir needs to be legitimate."

She was still confused. "Don't you have several mistresses all over the world tucked away?"

Harrison chuckled. "I'm flattered that you think I have that kind of stamina, but the truth is that I prefer to keep my business and pleasure separate. I need a wife that will give me a child within the next eighteen months."

Sierra blinked, wanting to ask if the wife was the business, or the pleasure part. But that part of her sense of humor was tamped down by the overwhelming burden of her brother's crimes. "I'm still not clear on how Daniel fits into this conversation."

He stood up and stirred the bean soup that had started to sizzle on the stove. "It's simple. You become my wife, give me an heir and I won't prosecute your brother for theft and other crimes."

He sat down again, watching her beautiful features as she slowly absorbed his offer. She really was exceptionally lovely, he thought. Not even the hardships of the past three years could diminish the softness of her skin or the sheen of her hair.

He'd like it down around her shoulders though, instead of tied up on the back of her head. He wasn't sure about her figure, but if anything, she was more slender now than she was before. The bulky clothes she preferred now were most likely her way of blending into the woodwork. He suspected that she'd ignored all of the colorful clothing that had made her stand out in the past, preferring clothing that wasn't so obvious. But what she didn't understand was that beauty like hers couldn't be hidden. It stood out like a beacon, pulling one's eyes towards her delicate features and the elegant way she had about her.

That was all going to have to stop, he thought silently. The dark, bulky clothes, the tentative expression…. He wasn't going to allow her to hide. No, a woman with her beauty needed to be showcased. She should be celebrated. And…she should be in his bed. Just like she should have been for the past three years.

Yes, this woman was lovely and, he suspected, sensuous if that one kiss between them was any indication. Once he showed her how to release her inhibitions, he knew she would be a fantastic lover. This was all going to work out perfectly, he thought with triumph.

He was watching her carefully and his body hardened involuntarily when her sexy tongue darted out to lick her lips. He wanted to capture those lips again, taste her and feel her come alive under his hands just like she had that one time three years ago. Damn, but she had been amazing to feel. She had been like holding a lightning bolt.

"Let me get this straight," she said and pushed a wisp of dark, blond hair behind her ear. "You need an heir and you want me to produce it for you. And in return, you won't press charges against my brother."

"I believe that is what I have stated."

She was silent for another long moment, her fingers clenching and unclenching around the cup of tea. "And this heir needs to be legitimate."

He nodded. "Yes."

She took a deep breath, holding the cup tightly. She worked through the mechanics in her mind and came to the only logical conclusion. "You want me to marry you."

He shrugged his shoulder. "You were ready to marry a man you didn't love before. The only difference now is that you would be doing it for your brother and not for your father's business."

That sounded so crass and she stiffened. "I wasn't marrying Evan for my father's business."

He looked at her skeptically. "Evan was the son of one of your father's major clients. Of course you were marrying the boy for his connections."

Sierra hadn't heard that before. It was all more of a blur now, her mind preferring to push that horrible time from her past away. Had Evan really been connected in that way? Had her father given Evan a job simply as a way to appease one of his clients? She'd always felt horrible about the engagement, but this news added a whole new layer of disgust to the relationship. But the reality was so much worse, she realized suddenly. Evan hadn't cared for her in any way. He'd only been marrying her because he'd wanted a job! A good job in one of the top investment firms and he'd done it by dating the owner's daughter! How pathetic!

Harrison had no idea what was going through her mind as he stood up, putting a business card on the table in front of her. "Think about it and meet me at my office tomorrow. I'll expect your answer by then." He closed up his laptop and walked to the door. "If you decide not to accept my offer, then the police will be at your door by five o'clock tomorrow evening. And I suspect they will be interested to know that you didn't seem overly surprised by the activities on the video. Obstruction of justice and abetting a criminal are also prosecutable offenses, Sierra."

A moment later, the door closed on her misery and Sierra dropped her head onto her hands as she lost the battle for control of her emotions. The sobs broke through the silence of the kitchen, tearing her up inside as fear, anger, desperation and disgust threatened to choke her.

Damn him! And damn Daniel as well! The kid was angry, she understood that! But for him to do this! To steal valuables! And then to drag her into the muck just when she was starting to figure out her life and find a small measure of happiness! She'd tried to be compassionate about his antics, to understand her younger brother but she was so terrified, so overwhelmed and confused about the right path.

Sierra couldn't eat that night. She poured the bean soup into a container, hoping it would be a hearty meal when she finally was able to stomach food once again. Nor could she sleep that night. Every sound, every creak in the old cottage sounded like either Daniel coming back home or someone trying to sneak into the house to get her. Why someone would even venture into such an old house, she couldn't rationalize but her mind was exhausted from trying to figure out a way to resolve all of these issues and coming up blank.

When her alarm went off the following morning, her whole body ached from the stress from both Daniel's actions, the threat of him being arrested, and the only solution she could come up with that would solve all of the problems – accepting Harrison's proposal. It sounded crazy, but nothing else occurred to her. She wished she could pay him back, or maybe even just beg him to pretend Daniel hadn't stolen the items. But she suspected that Daniel still hadn't returned the items. He'd been too furious with her when he'd stormed out the last time.

But she had to face the world. As much as she'd like to just pull the pillow over her head and pretend the day hadn't started, she couldn't ignore reality.

When she reported for work that morning, she found that she was in for yet another stunning surprise.

"Sierra, what are you doing here? Shouldn't you be up at the main house taking it easy?" Bob, her boss, suggested.

Sierra stared at the older man, not sure what he meant but pretty sure that it couldn't be good. "Why would I be at the main house?" she asked, rubbing her hand down the nose of one of the horses as she passed by his stall. They were all affectionate guys, wanting a pet or a scratch. Most of the time they were out in the pasture but came in to the stables during feeding times.

Bob shuffled past, pouring grain into each of the feed bins, normally a job that Sierra did while he was checking things out. "His Grace called earlier. He said you were to take the day off. You were supposed to report up to the house for some reason. Not sure why though. Ruth might have more information." Bob shrugged as if whatever was going on was none of his business. When the horses were fed, he moved on down to the office.

Sierra walked up the hill to the main house, her body trembling as she contemplated all of the possibilities. All of them ended with a tall, terrifying man who could kiss her until her senses swirled. At least, he used to be able to do that. Maybe it had only been that one time, she told herself as she pulled open the kitchen door and peered inside, feeling like an intruder even though she'd spent the majority of her life here. She hadn't stepped through this door in three years though. Not since she and Daniel had been evicted. And she refused to look over at the patio, that place where Harrison had kissed her that night.

She couldn't imagine what responsibilities she might have here but she slipped through the side door that would lead to the kitchen. "Hi Ruth. Bob told me that I was to report here this morning. Do you need help?" she asked as she pulled off her leather work gloves and wool hat. She tried smoothing her sandy-blond hair down, but it was pointless after wearing that hat. Not to mention, she hadn't slept well last night, tossing and turning in her lumpy bed just trying to figure out what she was going to do about the man's proposal, Daniel's whereabouts, her job, her classes and how she was going to pay the rent this month if she had additional legal bills to pay because of Daniel's impetuous and stupid idea for getting them out of debt.

Ruth looked over at Sierra and smiled warmly. Both Bob and Ruth had never made her feel horrible for her father's arrest or her mother's suicide. They'd been with the family for a long time and were always kind.

"His Grace is in the dining room," Ruth explained with a bright smile. "He said that you might want to have breakfast with him to discuss any other questions you might have about your engagement." She lifted the teapot and carried it over to the sink. "I had no idea you were seeing the man but I'm thrilled that you're finally dating again. It's been so hard for both you and Daniel. I'm glad that things are starting to finally turn around for you."

Sierra froze at the explanation, not sure she'd heard the housekeeper correctly. "Did he actually say those words? That he and I were engaged?"

Ruth turned on the stove. "Oh, yes. He even had a man here last night with engagement rings." She winked at Sierra. "I hope I'm not spoiling the surprise, but I took a peek. You're going to love the one he chose!"

Ruth bustled about her business, making tea and setting everything on a tray. All the while, Sierra stood near the doorway, her mind going over their conversation from the previous night. At no point had she ever agreed to that man's offer! But here he was, basically announcing it to the world since Ruth would definitely talk about the news when she went to the market later today.

She was furious! For years before her father's arrest, she'd been sleep walking through life. But after all she'd been through, she'd grown up, she'd come alive. Yes, a lot of that living had been painful, but she was no longer coasting along, letting others make decisions for her.

And there was no way this arrogant man was going to change that for her! He might be gorgeous and handsome and…okay, so he kissed better than she'd thought possible. But still…

She was the ruler of her destiny! She simply would not allow this man to step into her life and make decisions for her! He'd given her until tonight to make a choice. Darn him! He was not following through!

Walking into the breakfast room, she found Harrison sitting at the head of the table, sunshine streaming over his black hair and bouncing off of the newspaper he was reading. He looked shockingly handsome and so powerful, his presence sent a shiver of awareness throughout her whole body. Her mind flashed back to that moment at the party, the exact moment when he'd walked into the house, when their eyes had clashed. Even then, he'd had this impact on her. And it was going to stop!

Staring at him as he lifted the delicate china cup to his firm lips, she felt a shudder tear through her. This was not happening, she told herself. He was not controlling her simply with his eyes! Besides, she'd seen this picture so many times while growing up and her heart ached. But that had been her father sitting there. Not the man who had become enemy number one.

"I can't do it," she told him, her chin lifting up defiantly.

He didn't even lift his eyes from the newspaper. "Sit down, Sierra," he told her, ignoring her rejection. "Ruth is bringing hot coffee. Have something to eat."

She continued to stand in the doorway until Ruth came up behind her. "Oh dear, I'll have to get you another cup, won't I? Weren't expecting you, Your Grace!" she gushed. "Not that we aren't thrilled to have you. It is always exciting

37

when you come to stay for a few days. Especially exciting this time with the great news and all."

And with those words she bustled out, eager to do her part in urging on the budding romance.

Sierra's body was practically vibrating with fury. Or at least, that's the emotion she was claiming. She wouldn't admit, even to herself, that this man excited her as no other man ever had. She glared at him even though he still wasn't looking at her. "How could you have told Ruth that we are getting married?" she demanded.

Harrison the quiver in her chin and had to fight his instinct to pull her into his arms and tell her that everything was going to be okay, that he would make it okay. He turned the page in the newspaper, scanning the articles and firming up his resolve. "Because we are. You don't really have a choice in the matter." He looked up and those blue eyes chilled her with that implacable glance. "Do you?"

The trembling increased because no, she didn't really have a choice. "I didn't do anything wrong. I won't be arrested. You won't do that to me." She had no idea if he would follow through on his threat to have her arrested for…what were his words? Aiding and abetting a criminal? No, she looked at him across the table, he wouldn't have her arrested.

Would he?

She didn't know this man except that he kissed like…well, she wasn't thinking about that kiss. Ever! Darn it, how many times did she have to tell herself that before she finally accepted it?

Harrison looked up and watched the woman, noticing that she was wearing yet another baggy sweater and a canvas coat that hid her figure from her neck almost to her knees. "Take off that jacket, Sierra. Sit down before you fall down. You look like a gust of wind could topple you over."

And to make sure that she followed his orders, he walked over to her and took her hand, leading her to the chair directly next to his. He took the additional cup Ruth had just brought in and set it down in front of her, pouring her the brew himself.

"Thank you, Ruth. That will be all." And he dismissed the housekeeper.

When they were once again alone, he sat down in his chair and looked at her. "You'll have to stop wearing clothes like that."

She looked down at her coat and worn out sweater, cringing at how pathetic she must appear. She wasn't going to admit to this man that she now felt self-conscious in the shapeless clothing. "I prefer these clothes. They suit me better."

He sipped his coffee before setting it back down in the saucer. "You prefer to hide from the world in those clothes. But as my duchess, you won't be able to do that. The press is continuously photographing me and you can't look like a homeless person. You'll get a new wardrobe immediately."

She pulled the canvas closer. "I haven't agreed to marry you. You gave me until five o'clock tonight to make a decision."

He folded the newspaper and set it to the side, firmly reining in his body's reaction to her bristling anger. She really was a stunning beauty, he thought. And her defiance, her pride only made her more fascinating. He didn't want to crush her spirit, especially since it was so new to her, but he had to get her out of this mess. Besides, he knew that the sexual chemistry was still there between them, stronger actually. She was fighting it for some reason, but he would overcome her objections somehow. "Yes, but since we both know that you will agree to my terms, let's just move on with the details until then, shall we?"

Sierra gritted her teeth, wanting so badly to give him a firm set-down. But she didn't dare. She had no idea what this man might do to her. She suspected that he truly was as ruthless as his reputation indicated and wouldn't hesitate to have both her and her brother arrested. Now that she was sitting next to him, she could see the ruthlessness in his eyes, the lack of mercy.

She shifted uncomfortably in her chair. "I think obtaining a new wardrobe is premature. Besides, I don't have the money for new clothes. These will simply have to do or you can find another woman to..." She couldn't say the words, thinking it was too intimate of a subject. They barely knew each other! They'd spoken only a few sentences.

"I think not," he stated firmly. "You'll need to get something done with that hair as well. As lovely as it is, you can't be wearing it back in that band all the time either."

Her hand lifted to her hair self-consciously. "What's wrong with my hair?"

"Nothing at all, my lovely lady. But you are about to become a duchess. And that requires a bit more finesse than your normal styling patterns. There are many functions in which I will need you by my side in order to convince the world that this is a legitimate union."

This was startling news. "What do you mean?" She didn't go out into society any longer. After her father's arrest, all of the invitations to social events had died out. Nor had she wanted to step out into the social whirl. She'd enjoyed not having to get her nails done every week, her sandy-blond hair trimmed and highlighted every month. And she'd enjoyed not having to keep up with the latest fashions. Before her world had crumbled, she'd spent disgusting amounts of time shopping. Not having to worry about things like that had freed up hours in her day, allowing her to study more, take care of the horses. It was so much more comfortable being invisible, she thought.

Harrison wasn't going to allow her to hide though. He was shoving her right back into the limelight. "I mean, I need a legitimate heir. I can't have any questions about the legitimacy of my son. So you will need to play the role of my loving wife to perfection. That means accompanying me on various outings, dinners, parties and things of that nature. My business is international, so there will be travel involved as well."

All of this was hitting her hard. She was having trouble processing all of the information he was tossing at her. It was too much! Last night, all she could think about was sharing a name with this man but now he was tossing so much more into the bargain. "I can't do this," she replied, feeling like the walls were closing in on her. "I can't handle all of it."

He wasn't letting her get away with that. "Of course you can," he challenged her. "I saw the pictures of you three years ago, Sierra. You were strong and defiant. Find that person again and lift your head. Regain your pride." He watched as her chin trembled slightly. "You were beautiful back then. The papers ridiculed your parents and yet, you stood up to all of them, shoulders back, your eyes rebellious. Find that person again. Show them that you're strong and beautiful once again." With that, he stood up. With a finger under her chin, he tilted her head back. "Bring back the woman who knows how to put a man in his place," he dared her.

With those words, he kissed her hard, then left her reeling with the impact of that kiss. "I have meetings but we'll meet at my office tonight. I've arranged for several designers to arrive here today. Pick out anything you like. Roger, your new bodyguard, also has the authority to take you shopping. You'll need to get your hair and nails done and," he looked at her features critically, "perhaps a bit of makeup? You're looking a little too pale for defiance, my love." With that, he lifted the jacket that had been resting on the back of his chair and slid it on. "We'll go out for dinner tonight to celebrate."

A moment later, he was gone, leaving Sierra to sift through all of his orders and try to think. The man was insane, she thought as she took a long, fortifying sip of her coffee. He'd stepped into her house last night and threatened her, then showed up this morning to give her a series of orders about her appearance.

She realized that she actually hated the man. From deep down inside of her, she felt a welling of hatred so strong, she couldn't believe it.

Just like the last time this man had come into her life, she'd realized that she'd been floating along. Unlike the last time though, she had goals and activities that she loved doing. She was making her way in the world on her own.

But she hadn't felt this strongly, this passionately about another person, about anything, actually, in ages! If ever!

Standing up, she forced a smile for Ruth who was bringing in a large platter of eggs and fresh coffee as well as a basket filled with muffins. "Now don't you dare leave this table without eating anything, Ms. Sierra," she said and bustled into the room. "Believe me, after serving him for the past three years, you are going to need your strength. I know that you are a skinny, little thing, but you're going to need every ounce of energy you can dig up inside of you. He's a demanding man, I'll tell you that much!" she said and shook her head as she bustled back out of the room.

Sierra looked down at the veritable feast on the table. Yes, she was suddenly hungry. And Ruth was completely right. She would need her strength to fight Harrison Aimsworth, Duke of Selton. The man was horrible, despicable and arrogant. And she felt more alive now with this hatred flowing through her than she had in so long!

She ate more than half of the eggs and two of the muffins, downing additional cups of coffee. When she stood up again, she felt revived! And ready to battle the man in question.

She was just about to walk out of the house when the doorbell rang. She had no business wondering who it might be, but Ruth suspected. "That must be the people that are bringing you new clothes," she said, clapping her hands in excitement. "Oh, goodness, it will be so wonderful to have you back in the house, miss! And as a duchess, this time!" She hurried out of the room, excited to answer the front door.

Sierra thought about walking out, leaving whoever was at the front door and not even caring. But then a thought struck her. The man had organized designers to arrive? She would show him! The man was a conceited beast and she would order whatever she pleased. No limit? She'd show him what she could do with an unlimited budget!

Several men and women pushed in racks of hanging clothes and, when they pulled back the covers, Sierra gasped at the beautiful dresses, blouses, slacks, skirts and everything in between. "Oh my," she whispered with growing excitement.

"Lord Aimsworth asked that I assist you with your choices," a lady moved over to stand next to Sierra. "Perhaps we should start with dresses?" she suggested. "A V neck style would be best for your figure."

Sierra looked at the woman who had dared to look disparagingly at her canvas coat and bulky clothes. Something shifted inside of her, a force that she hadn't felt in so long, it sort of felt foreign. But good! "Actually, I don't have large enough breasts to handle a V neck," Sierra replied with an overly sweet tone. "My figure looks better with a boat neck or, if anything is available in a wrap style, that would be even more flattering." She dismissed the woman who was obviously a personal shopper and turned to the others. "Show me what you've got," she said.

The others snapped into action, ignoring the lady who had obviously been dismissed. Everyone seemed more than eager to cater to the needs of the future Duchess of Selton. Sierra had never really cared a whole lot about titles. Her father and mother had been obsessed about their clients and which of them had titles but she'd never really thought that a title made a person better.

41

But the idea of having people cater to her like this, after three years of hideous treatment and suspicion, sometimes outright anger by the villagers and local craftspeople, it felt good.

She went through the clothes for two hours and bought anything she wanted. When another knock on the door sounded, she opened it to find a hairdresser and makeup artist standing there, tools in hand and ready to help.

By the time four o'clock rolled around, she felt like a new person. She'd had several inches of her hair cut off and it now floated around her shoulders, her neck feeling much less burdened without the extra weight. The makeup person tried to convince Sierra to purchase several different colors and foundations, creams and the like, but Sierra knew how to make the best of her features. She just hadn't had a reason to do it in a long time. Nor had she found the energy. It was easier to simply go without. Oh, and there was the burdensome issue of money. As she'd worked in the stables and tried to keep a growing teenager fed, not to mention putting as much money towards education as she could, makeup expenditures had seemed silly.

So today, she stuck to minimalist makeup without all the extras, much to the chagrin of the departing artist.

Slipping into a soft, pink cashmere sweater dress that hugged her figure perfectly, she flipped her hair out again, letting it dance around her made up face. As she walked down the stairs, she pulled her phone out of her new purse that really only contained gloss and her cell phone. She hadn't carried a wallet around for months. She had no credit cards and didn't drive so she had no keys. She got around the village on her bike, preferring to save money that way.

Dialing Daniel's number, she waited in the back of the limousine, praying that her brother would finally pick up the phone.

When it once again went to voice mail, she pressed her lips together. "Daniel, it's me again. Please call me back. We urgently need to talk."

She didn't want him to hear about any of this over the phone.

Too quickly, the limousine pulled up outside of a massive sky rise with "Aimsworth Industries" on the outside. Seeing this newest indicator of Harrison's wealth and power, she was more than a little intimidated. As she followed the man named Roger, who was a large, bulky man with scary bulges on the sides of his suit, she wondered what it was that Harrison actually did for a living. Three years ago, she'd simply assumed he was an indolent aristocrat, living off of the rents of his tenants or inherited money. She'd never imagined that the man was a productive member of the business world, although she should have suspected as much with his demeanor. But this building, and all of the employees rushing around with "Aimsworth Industries" badges attached to their lapels, looked much more businesslike. It put him into a different realm altogether. Good grief, wasn't it enough that the man held the title of duke? Couldn't he be…boring? Or irritating? Fat? Obnoxious? Okay, well, he really was obnoxious. And arrogant.

She was procrastinating. The man assigned as her bodyguard was looking at her curiously since she was simply standing in front of the massive, steel and glass skyscraper, looking up and not moving forward. Everyone on the sidewalk was having to move around her, some of them glaring at her with irritation. The guard was obviously anxious to get her into the building and to safety. Sierra was just as anxious to stay out of that building. Away from Harrison's more obvious symbol of power.

Was the man really that brilliant? The only knowledge she had of him was when she allowed herself to flip through the tabloids while waiting in line at the grocery store. She knew that he'd had a stream of mistresses or beautiful women on his arm. The man really was a womanizer, her present predicament adding only more credence that he deserved that moniker.

"We need to move, Ms. Warner," her guard urged, his big body blocking the other pedestrians from bumping into her.

Sierra sighed. "Yes. Fine," and she reluctantly followed the man through the heavy glass doors.

Roger had arranged for her to be whisked up to the executive floor without needing to go through security so she was standing outside of Harrison's office doors much more quickly than she'd anticipated.

As she stood there, her hand hesitating to knock on the double doors, she smoothed the dress down over her hips. What was she doing? She couldn't go through with this!

She was just about to turn around when the door was opened from the inside. Harrison stood there, staring down at her as he spoke to someone who was obviously on speakerphone.

For a long moment, neither of them said a word. She simply stared at him and he looked down at her with an odd gleam to his eyes. She was just about to turn around and run away when he firmly took her hand and pulled her into his office, slamming the door behind him. He walked over to a wall and pressed a button, speaking in French the whole time. A hidden bar appeared and he reached into the small refrigerator and pulled out a bottle of white wine, pouring her a glass. As soon as he handed it to her, he walked back and poured himself something that looked suspiciously like scotch but she had no idea what it really was. Nor did she know the difference between scotch, whiskey, bourbon or any other strange brew that men seemed to prefer. They all sounded abominably foul to her and she couldn't stomach any cocktail made with them.

She watched with fascination as he threw back his portion of whatever it was and poured himself another before pressing the button once again, making the bar disappear.

The entire time, he maintained the conversation and she wished she could remember enough of her French to understand what he was saying.

When the phone call ended, the shivering started up full force. This was such a bad idea, she thought as the man looked at her from the other side of his desk. She was no match for this man. She was probably better off in jail. At least there she'd be protected from the heat that was in his eyes as he looked at her.

"You look better," he finally said, breaking the silence.

Her mouth fell open with that lame compliment. "Better?" she demanded furiously, her head and shoulders going back with the word.

He chuckled and leaned back against his desk. "You look lovely. Is that more soothing to your ruffled feathers, my lady?" He loved seeing the fire back in her silver eyes. He'd been concerned when she'd walked into the breakfast room this morning. She looked almost sick with pale skin and trembling arms and limbs. He'd had to fight the urge to take her into his arms and tell her that he would take care of her.

Sierra didn't answer his question but he moved closer, enjoying her soft, feminine scent.

"We need to talk," she told him firmly. "I'm not going into this blindly as you think is going to happen."

"On the contrary," he told her and reached behind him to a file folder. "Here is a prenuptial contract, stating the terms of our marriage as well as a generous annual amount to be given to you regardless of whether a child is born of this marriage."

Sierra opened the file folder and looked through the papers. She couldn't stop the gasp of surprise at the amount he would be providing for her. "That's too much," she told him, handing it back to him. She realized that her words were implying that she was accepting his offer. Or maybe it was the fact that she'd allowed him to buy her clothes. Or perhaps it was simply her presence here. She wasn't exactly sure what she was feeling so trying to figure out what he might be thinking was way beyond her capabilities at the moment.

"Nonsense. You'll have earned it. And you'll get more if you are able to conceive and a child is born. I'm a very generous man."

"Is that your excuse for being such a horrible human being all the rest of the time?"

His smile twitched slightly. "Of course."

She sighed, realizing she wasn't going to score any points on him. "What happens to you if I don't conceive?" she asked, looking down and feeling more than a little exhausted.

"Don't worry about that."

Her head came up with those words. "But…"

He chuckled as her silver eyes lifted to his, worry obvious in her mind. "I'll do my best to ensure that you do conceive."

She blushed with those words but looked down at the papers. "How is that going to come about? Do you have a clinic in mind?"

His eyes shuttered with that question. He'd wanted to stipulate a doctor to care for her, but didn't want to presume anything. "I assumed you would prefer to stay with your own obstetrician."

She shook her head, pretending as if this issue wasn't as intimate as it felt. She was looking down at the floor, wishing she could be anywhere but here, discussing anything other than this intimate subject with this particular man. It seemed somehow…wrong…to be talking about artificial means of conceiving although she couldn't put her finger on what was so wrong about it. "I meant…do you have a clinic that will do the fertility? The mixing of the…things?"

He was silent for a moment, trying to figure out what she meant. What "things" needed to be mixed? Conceiving seemed like a very straightforward, and extremely enjoyable, endeavor in his mind. When he finally understood what she was asking, he laughed, enchanted with her rosy cheeks. "Ah, I get your meaning. But unfortunately for you, my beauty, I'm a traditional kind of guy. I think we should stick with the normal methods for conception. If things don't work out properly, we'll have enough time to visit fertility specialists."

Sierra's hands almost dropped the papers with that announcement. "We're going to…" she shook her head. "No. That's impossible."

He stood up and took the contract out of her hands. "It is not only possible, but very enjoyable. But it has probably been a while. I know that Evan Winters…broke things off with you after your father's arrest. But surely you've…"

He was asking if she'd taken another lover? Really?

She glanced up at his blue eyes, then away again, unable to hold his confident gaze. How could she tell this dynamic and overly sexy man that she'd never…that she and Evan hadn't…Oh, good grief! Could this be any more awkward?!

She shook her head and stood up as well, moving behind the chair. "No. This isn't going to work. I can't do it." Her hands were trembling so badly at the idea of having sex with this man that she hid them behind her back, not wanting him to know how much he could affect her.

Harrison's eyes narrowed as she started shivering once again. Was she really this timid? Deciding that it was time to bring out the big guns, he sighed and stood up, coming closer to her. Looking down at the top of her head, he announced, "Your brother is staying with his friend up in Uxbridge."

Sierra's breath halted and she stared up at him. He was so hard, so impenetrable. And how in the world did he know where her brother was when she couldn't even get Daniel to call her back? What resources did he have that would allow him to track down a teenage boy determined to hide away from his responsibilities? "Why are you doing this?" she asked desperately.

Harrison didn't answer her. Instead, he walked around the chair and took her into his arms. She held her breath as she realized what he was about to do. That one night three years ago flashed into her mind and she shivered as she watched his head descend to hers. She wanted to tell him not to kiss her, to not touch her in that way. It had messed with her sleep, her dreams and haunted her so many nights over the past three years. But the words wouldn't come. She couldn't say anything as she tensed, waiting for his touch.

And then it was there, his lips upon hers and everything else faded as his hands pulled her against his hard body, his mouth moved against hers, invading her mouth, invading her mind with the heated desire in his kiss. There was no tomorrow, no worries about her brother avoiding jail time and no stress about a wedding that would sweep her away, leaving her scared, confused and miserable.

It was just this kiss, this moment as he deepened the kiss, pulled her against him and his hands sliding down her body, back up her spine and causing her to know intimately what it was like to be held in his arms.

She realized several things in that moment. The man was not just tall, he was shockingly strong. Her fingers tightened around his arms, feeling the muscles underneath the tame material. That tailored shirt was hiding a physical strength that only added to the crazy mixture of lust and need that threatened to choke her with his kiss.

She also realized that her memories of the kiss three years ago were faulty. She hadn't remembered the heat, the hunger that drove her to press her body closer, move against him and cause her voice to whimper when she couldn't get close enough.

There was more, oh, so much more. But his hand slid higher, his fingers fisting in her hair as he pulled her head backwards. She leaned into him, her hands moving up his arms, reveling in his strength as her hands slowly moved higher, eventually wrapping around his neck to hold him against her.

Slowly, he lifted his head, his eyes looking down into hers with that triumph that she was slowly growing to hate about him. "And that would be why we're doing this the old fashioned way," he told her, lifting her back up and holding her until she was once again steady.

Chapter 4

"I now pronounce you husband and wife," the officiant said.

Sierra turned, facing the man who was now her husband. This wasn't happening, she thought even as his head dipped lower for the kiss. She shook her head slightly, her eyes wide and all she could think about was how angry she was at her brother for putting her into this position.

Everything had been fine! Okay, so he needed to find a job and go to school, figure out what he wanted to do with his future. But he shouldn't have…

And then she couldn't think at all. Just like the last time in his office, the moment his lips touched hers, all thoughts flew out of her head. The man knew how to kiss!

But this time, he didn't do the whole mind-melt thing. He lifted his head with just a simple, lingering kiss. Staring up at him with surprise, she couldn't believe he would do something so tame. She was…disappointed?

Absolutely not! She was relieved that he wasn't going to kiss her like that again! Especially in front of all of these strangers. She lost her head when Harrison kissed her and it was embarrassing. She was relieved that he hadn't been more demonstrative in front of people she didn't know.

There were only a handful of people, but they all applauded, slapping Harrison on the back while two beautiful ladies, one blond and one dark-haired woman, took her into a welcoming hug.

"Don't worry," the blond woman said as she hugged Sierra. "He's really not as bad as he seems. Just ignore him when he becomes too grumpy."

Harrison heard that comment and Sierra thought she heard her new husband growl. But that was impossible, wasn't it? The man didn't really growl. Wasn't he too dignified for something so…uncivilized?

The dark haired woman stepped up next and took Sierra's hands in hers. "I'm Sasha Galanos. I'm thrilled to meet you because Scarlett and I," she said, tilting her head to the blond woman, "are still outnumbered and need reinforcements against these horrible beasts." Sierra glanced at the strikingly handsome man behind Sasha. She would have laughed when the man rolled his eyes, but she was too nervous and confused. The woman continued, ignoring the glare from her husband. "I know what you're getting into and, believe me, you're going to need help. Just call me, okay? They are horrible men, but obviously you've learned to love him."

Sierra had no idea who this woman was, but she was strangely reassured from the two women's freely given words of support. She glanced up at her husband, still thinking that she was in shock. Or dreaming and she'd wake up and this would all go away.

She couldn't believe she was married to this man! Good grief, surely this was a nightmare. It just couldn't be real.

Her eyes moved around the room and found Harrison. He was surrounded by several other men, all of them about the same height and that woman, the blond one.

She took a deep breath, trying to regain control of her wavering resolve. This was going to be okay. Daniel would be okay and she was going to be okay. She'd make this okay.

But that kiss, she thought! Goodness, it had been just a slight touch, but it had still affected her deeply.

Harrison caught her eye and she shivered. She was a duchess now. Titles had never been important to her, but her mother had always wanted a title. Her mother had actually rejected her father's proposal initially because he'd had the money, but not the title. She used to tease him about that occasionally, but deep down, Sierra suspected that her mother hadn't been happy without the title. She'd wanted to be a lady.

Sierra's mother would be preening right now, knowing that her daughter was a duchess. A duchess? Okay, so that was intimidating but even worse, she was a wife? She was the wife to Harrison Aimsworth! How had her world so completely turned upside down?

She would never have to worry about money again. Or so he said. Sierra didn't believe that. There was no way she would ever put her financial future in another person's hands again. She'd thought that she'd been financially secure while her father was alive but look how that had turned out.

Sierra jumped about a foot when Harrison came up behind her. "What are you thinking about?" he asked, lifting her hand and kissing her fingers. Or at least, that's how it looked to the other guests. Sierra felt his teeth on her fingers and was startled by the fire that was ignited with such a seemingly simple touch.

"What are you doing?" she demanded.

His smile was slow and sexy and her stomach muscles tightened with anticipation. And dread? As she looked up at him, she wished that there was dread but...

"You look too pale. Have some champagne and relax."

He didn't take no for an answer, tugging her gently over to the side table where a bartender was pouring drinks for the small group of guests.

"Who are these people?" she asked as she accepted the glass of sparkling wine but she didn't sip it.

"They're good friends," he told her, putting a hand around her waist and pulling her slightly closer. "I went to boarding school with them."

Her eyes slashed to the blond woman. "All of them?"

Harrison chuckled, realizing where her mind was going. "Scarlett, the blond woman, is like a kid sister to most of us."

"Most?" she clarified. She wanted to understand this man but he kept talking in riddles, as if she should know some secret code before she could comprehend his language.

Harrison's head bent down slightly and he lifted his own glass, indicating the bold, dark haired American man standing close to the blond woman. They almost looked like a couple except they would scowl at each other occasionally. "The man there is Grayson Brooks and he's madly in love with Scarlett Evans. Has been since he was about twenty-five years old. But he won't do anything about it."

Sierra was painfully aware of Harrison's large body right next to hers and she resisted the strange impulse to lean into his side. Why did she feel the urge to lay her head against his hard shoulder? She shook her head and tried very hard to focus on what he was saying. "If he's been in love with her for that long, why hasn't he done anything about it?"

She sensed as well as felt her new husband's laughter. It was very low and Sierra suspected that she was the only one who heard it. "Because they prefer to battle things out instead. But we're going to have to do something about that soon."

Sierra looked up into his blue eyes, wondering what he meant. But it was yet another riddle. "Okay, so who are the other people?"

Harrison moved to the next man. "Malik Amari del Nader," he said and heard Sierra's gasp of recognition. "You're correct. He's the Sheik of Sarkit."

"You're friends with a sheik?" she asked, awed and more than a little impressed.

Harrison rolled his eyes. "I can take him down," he told her, irritated that the other man was getting more respect than she was willing to give his own title.

Sierra laughed softly and Harrison thrilled to the sound. He hadn't heard her sweet, musical laugh since that night three years ago and it was a lovely sound.

"I'm sure you can," she assured him, reaching out to pat his chest. He glanced down at her, startled as his body hardened even more. He didn't think she even realized what she was doing but, since it was the first time she'd willingly touched him, he was fully aware. And his body throbbed, needing to get her alone.

He turned his attention to the next man. "Damon Galanos and his wife Sasha. They have actually been married for more than six years."

Scarlett's eyes widened. "They look like newlyweds," she mentioned, thinking that the way they were touching was very sweet. Both of them needed to be close to each other, a bit like the blond and the American but those two didn't touch. The dark haired woman with the sultry eyes couldn't seem to keep her hands off of her husband and he wouldn't let her out of his sight.

"In a way, that's true. He married her, but…well, suffice it to say, they really only found each other a few months ago."

Sierra smiled. "It sounds very romantic."

Harrison grunted as he took a sip of his champagne. "I doubt Damon would agree with your assessment."

She laughed again. "Men never do."

His hand tightened on her waist with the sound but he slowly released her. There would be plenty of time tonight to touch her. And he planned on knowing where every spot on her body was that turned her on by the time morning arrived.

"The other guy is Stefan Kozlov."

Sierra's eyes slashed up to his. "Why do I know that name?"

Harrison shrugged. "I couldn't tell you." His eyes turned blank, not wanting to discuss his friend's troubles.

Sierra struggled to place the name and the face and then she gasped. "Wasn't he married just a few months ago? It was some fabulous wedding with hundreds of guests but the bride disappeared on their wedding day. Is that the same man?" She'd read about that in the tabloids while checking out at the grocery store.

Harrison only looked down at his new wife, not saying a word. Sierra instantly understood and smiled brightly. "You certainly have an interesting group of friends, Harrison Aimsworth," she commented.

He turned her around so that she was facing him. "And you invited none of your friends to the wedding, Ms. Aimsworth. Why is that?" he asked softly but with a tone that suggested he wasn't happy about it.

Sierra's lashes lowered and she shrugged her lace-covered shoulder. "I didn't really…" how could she tell the man that her only friends were servants? Ruth and Bob were her friends, a couple of shop owners…but she hadn't felt comfortable inviting them to this wedding. First of all, it was only a temporary marriage. Once she gave this man his heir, the two of them would go their separate ways. It was entirely possible that she would be divorced in nine months. But secondly, Ruth and

Bob, her closest friends, were in this man's employ. They wouldn't dare attend the wedding of the Duke of Selton! It was unheard of! Impossible, in their minds. In hers as well. She conceded that, the only reason she was here was because she was the bride. Sierra was ninety-nine percent sure that no one in this beautiful room, besides her new husband, knew that she was the daughter of an accused embezzler and the sister of a thief. If they knew, she suspected that they wouldn't be as welcoming.

Harrison sighed. "Are you still having trouble in the village because of your father's arrest?"

That and because of the boys Daniel hung around, she thought. "It's okay. I have friends. They just wouldn't feel comfortable being here." She touched the middle of his chest again, trying to reassure him but as soon as she realized what she was doing, she whipped her hand away. Looking up into his blue eyes, she saw the instant heat and her breath caught in her throat.

"Very soon, Sierra, you will be doing that to me without these clothes on."

She shook her head. "Don't say things like that!" she gasped.

"Why?" he smiled triumphantly. "It is true," he countered.

"Stop it right now!" Stefan laughed. "The staff is waiting to serve dinner and I for one am starving!"

The others all laughed as well, obviously agreeing with the dangerous looking man. Sierra blushed but her eyes skimmed across the group. Saying one of them in particular was the "dangerous-looking" one was not helpful. All of them looked like they would come out of an alley fight the winner. Except for Harrison, she thought. He was elegant and strong, but he appeared to be above all the rambunctiousness.

"So the four of you got into some scrapes as teenagers, I understand?" she asked, sitting down in the chair Harrison was holding for her.

The four men stared at her for a long, pregnant moment before they glanced over at Harrison who was sitting down, unbuttoning his dark jacket and looking like he completely agreed with her.

But in the next moment, all five of them, including the blond woman but minus the dark haired beauty next to Damon Galanos, burst out laughing. Harrison only raised a dark eyebrow, still appearing detached from the conversation.

"Is that what your husband told you?" Malik asked as he finally stopped laughing. "If so, I hate to inform you of this, but your husband was the instigator of at least twenty percent of the fights among us. He had an annoying habit of issuing set-downs that only took an instant for us to be fighting it out."

Sierra stared at the man, not sure if he was teasing her or not. So she turned and looked up at her husband. When she saw that supercilious eyebrow go up, she knew that the man was speaking the truth. "You participated in the fights?" she gasped, still not sure she believed the man. She just couldn't picture Harrison

Aimsworth, Duke of Selton and businessman extraordinaire, participating in a fistfight! "How daring of you," she smiled.

The idea of Harrison battling it out with his fists was a new and interesting side of his personality. It somehow made him much more approachable.

"You'd be surprised what I can do with my hands," he replied, completely changing the subject.

Sierra stared at him blankly for a moment, but when that damnable heat entered his eyes, she blushed as he laughed softly. Lowering her lashes, she tried to fight the butterflies that fluttered through her stomach at the idea.

The rest of the dinner passed without incident. But no matter how hard she tried, she could not make the meal last longer. All of her hostess skills were useless as these men and women slowly stood up, preparing to leave almost immediately after the meal was finished. It was as if the others were all trying to get out of the room as quickly as possible and she noticed several quick looks from the men to her new husband.

"We have to go," Damon said, he and his beautiful wife being the last of them.

Sasha smiled up at him even as she took Sierra's hands. "Don't worry about anything," she told Sierra. "Harrison is a good man. I haven't known him long, but…"

Damon squeezed her gently, interrupting her. "She knows that, love. We have to go. They want to be alone."

Sasha laughed and allowed her husband to pull her away even while Sierra frantically searched her brain for a way to keep the kind woman here.

But the door shut on their departure before she could come up with a reasonable idea. And then she was alone with her husband. There was no noise except for her frantic breathing.

"Why did they have to leave so suddenly?" she asked, staring at the closed door. But she knew! They all had the same look on their faces, a look that told them that they knew what Harrison was going to do.

He confirmed her suspicions with his next words. "Because they knew that I wanted to be alone with my wife," he told her. He poured another glass of champagne and brought it over to her. "You barely ate anything during dinner, Sierra. Relax," and he took her hand, leading her through another set of doors and she gasped when she saw the beautiful suite. "I thought that was just one of the hotel's dining rooms," she whispered through stiff lips. It wasn't just a dining room. The double doors opened to a large suite filled with beautiful furniture and, on the opposite side of the suite, through another set of double doors, was the bedroom complete with an enormous bed.

"I suspected as much," he said as he laughed softly.

She resisted his pull but it didn't do much good. He was stronger and more determined. "Shouldn't we just...maybe hold off on that portion of our agreement? Just until we get to know each other a bit better?" She looked up at him with pleading eyes. "I mean, you only proposed this marriage idea a week ago and, since then, we've had two lunches together and one dinner. I barely know you."

He smiled slightly. "We're going to get to know each other much better tonight, Sierra." He knew she was nervous. But she was beautiful and she was his wife. He'd never thought he would get married until the idea occurred to him that she would make the ideal candidate to fulfill the requirements of his title. And even then, it had only made sense when he'd seen the evidence of her brother's crime.

"Do you have any idea how many times over the past three years that I came out to the house, wanting to take you out to dinner, Sierra?" he asked her as he finally got her into the bedroom.

She shook her head. "I was busy," she told him, trying to smother the trembling.

"You were hiding from me," he countered, turning her around so that his fingers could release the buttons that were going down the back of her tea-length wedding gown.

"I wasn't..." she couldn't finish the sentence because he'd released enough of the buttons that his strong fingers could touch the skin on her back and she gasped at the contact.

More buttons came undone and his fingers left a trail of fire down her spine. She was having trouble holding herself upright and she grabbed onto the only solid option – which just happened to be his hard thighs. When she realized what she'd grabbed, she whipped her hands away, clutching them against her chest.

Harrison laughed softly, lowering his head to kiss the nape of her neck. "You are allowed to touch me, Sierra. In fact, I like it. A lot."

She shook her head, holding the dress that felt like it was about to fall off of her shoulders.

He kissed the other side of her neck. "You're going to touch me eventually," he promised. Another kiss, this time on her spine causing her to gasp and arch away from his lips. "And you're going to like it just as much as I will." Another denial, but she had to close her eyes this time as the shiver still whipped through her.

"We should talk about this, Harrison." Another kiss, lower this time. "Please...couldn't we just..."

"We can talk," he promised, but his hands didn't stop unbuttoning the string of pearl buttons. His hands were now low on her back, almost touching her bottom. "Talk to me, Sierra. Tell me what you like. Tell me how you want me to touch you."

She had no idea what he meant by that! She hated it, but she loved the way he was touching her right now! No matter how much she wanted to deny it, her body absolutely loved the way his fingers trailed down her back. Sierra hadn't ever heard of a person's back being so sensitive, but hers was on fire from his fingers touching her.

"Oh please," she begged, her mind not sure what was going on. All she knew was that strange things were happening to her and she couldn't figure out if she liked it or wanted him to stop. She suspected that she would be very angry if he stopped, but shouldn't she want him to stop? Shouldn't she be begging him to stop?

This was crazy! How could he make her feel like this? She felt like her whole body was on fire!

Harrison watched the woman in his arms, his body throbbing with pain and pleasure at the way she instantly responded to his touch. He wanted to bend her over the bed and push himself into her heat but, at the same time, he wanted to take his time. This was their first time together. He wanted it slow. He wanted her to remember this time with him. For some reason, he needed to banish from her memory all the other men who had ever touched her delectable body. He wanted to be the only man who she thought of when he entered her for the first time.

"Lower your arms, Sierra," he coaxed even as his hands moved around to her stomach. He felt her stomach muscles contract and her body shiver but he didn't relent. Moving higher, he felt the stitching of her demi bra and almost groaned with the need to see her delicate body in the white lace. She'd truly gone all out with her undergarments and he was as eager as a school boy on his first date.

"I can't," she replied, clutching at the material to hold it over her breasts. "I can't let go."

He turned her around and bent lower, his lips capturing hers. At the first touch of his mouth against hers, she gasped, her eyes wide as she looked up at him. But a moment later, she wanted more. Reaching up with one hand while the other still clutched her dress, she lifted higher onto her toes and kissed him. Really kissed him. When his tongue demanded entry, she opened her mouth, reveling in the sensuousness of his kiss.

She wasn't aware of her body moving closer, of her breasts pressing against his chest or the way his arm wrapped around her waist, pulling her against his body but she was completely aware of the pressure against her stomach even if she didn't fully understand what it meant. All she knew was that this man was kissing her and making her feel those strange things, feelings she couldn't seem to control and, when his hand moved against her bottom, pulling her harder against his hips, she whimpered, not wanting him to stop.

Harrison lifted her hands away from the dress and almost growled with triumph when the lace fell to the floor, pooling at their feet. But he was too intent to see her, all of her. Lifting her out of the dress, she wasn't even aware of him kicking her wedding dress out of the way. He wasn't thinking of saving the dress for his future children or making sure that the lace didn't tear. All he could think about was getting this woman that had haunted him for three years into the bed so he could make love to her properly. And slowly.

But slowly wasn't coming to him. He felt her breasts against his chest as he lifted her into his arms, carrying her the last few feet to the bed. When he laid her down, his mouth didn't leave hers, his tongue mating with hers just as he wanted the rest of his body to do.

The urge to see her, to view her soft breasts and slim figure was too intense. He couldn't hold back and lifted away from her, his eyes looking down at the white lace that could barely hold those magnificent breasts. He noticed that her nipples were peeking through the lace and he bent down, his mouth taking the nipple through the delicate material. He didn't even have the energy to figure out how to release the catch on her bra.

When she arched into his mouth, he wanted more. His fingers pulled the material lower and his mouth, his teeth, nibbled on the budded flesh. He heard her gasp and wanted another one. With her fingers in his hair now, he lifted his head and looked down at her perfect body. Moving to the other breast, he gave that nipple the same attention. But when he heard her cry of passion, it inflamed him to heights he hadn't thought possible. He had to have her! He had to be inside of her.

Pulling out of her arms, he stood up and ripped his clothes off. Gone was the desire to make love to her slowly and thoroughly. He'd do that next. Right now, as he looked down at her writhing body, all he could think about was getting inside of her, feeling her heat wrap around his hard length and feeling her move against him. He tore his clothes off, tossing them to the side, uncaring about the cost of his suit in his need to feel her skin against his, to feel her body moving against him without any hindrance.

With a swift rip, her lace underwear was torn off of her. He thought he'd gone too far, too fast with that move but the look in her eyes told him otherwise. He relentlessly pulled her legs apart, looking down at her body, noticing how wet she was. He'd meant only to make room for himself, but when her hips moved, instinctively lifting and offering herself to him, he couldn't stop himself from bending lower and tasting her.

And when he felt her flesh against his tongue, his small taste turned into a feast. He couldn't get enough of her. Even when her hips tried to pull away from his mouth, he grabbed hold of her and kept her there, loving her scent and the taste of her. He heard her scream and felt her body convulse and was almost angry that her climax had come so quickly. But he assured himself that he would have plenty of time to explore her desire again in the future.

Sierra couldn't believe the incredible pleasure that pulsed through her. Nor could she work up a righteous anger about how he'd done that to her. All she could think was that she wanted that to happen again. Oh, not the first part. No, she hadn't liked the desperate way he'd made her feel or the clawing, driving need to find that elusive something. But when she'd discovered that "something" was the mind-blowing pleasure that was still throbbing through her as he moved over her, she could only smile, her body unable to even shift away from him. Perhaps a real lady would pull the covers over her nakedness, but she didn't even have the strength to do that.

But now he was kissing her stomach again. Why was he nibbling at her waist? Oh no, it was starting up again, she thought. "Please not again," she begged, but her limbs were weak and it was hard to stop him when he wanted to do something.

"Oh yes, my beauty. It still isn't over," he promised.

She shook her head, her hair tangling on the comforter behind her and she tried to pull backwards but Harrison wasn't allowing that. He lowered his body over hers, pinning the lower half of her with his legs. "Why shy away from this now?" he laughed softly even as his mouth latched onto her breast again.

She gasped when she felt that hardness probing lower on her body. "Harrison, I think I should…" she gasped when he pressed into her heat and it felt so perfect, so wonderful, that her mouth fell open. She forgot what she was going to tell him. He moved out and her eyes flew open, her hands moved to his hips, trying to pull him back into her body but he came back on his own and her hips lifted, meeting him. But it wasn't enough! Those crazy feelings, the rush of desperate need was swamping over her.

She needed more of him. It wasn't enough, this teasing and she wanted…more of all of him! "I can't…you…"

"Tell me what you want," he urged even as he pressed deeper into her heat, gritting his teeth to keep himself from slamming into her. She felt so perfect but she was tight! Almost too tight!

"Relax, Sierra," he urged, bending lower to kiss her. And with his kiss, he filled her up. At that same moment, he felt the barrier break and was stunned. Lifting his head, he saw the tear form in her closed eyes.

"Sierra?" he said her name as a question, still not sure if he believed what he'd just felt. "Are you a virgin?" he asked her gently.

Sierra kept her eyes closed as the pain slowly eased out of her body. Biting her lower lip to keep from sobbing, she shook her head. "Not anymore," she whispered. "Please, Harrison, this isn't comfortable anymore."

Harrison heard her words and wasn't sure what to do. He shifted ever so slightly and saw her eyes fly open. With a deep sigh of relief, he realized that she wasn't in so much pain any longer. "Are you okay?" he asked.

Sierra looked up at him, shocked at how good that slight movement felt. But she shook her head, her hands trying to keep his hips still. "No. Don't..." but he did! He moved and all those crazy feelings shot through her body. Shaking her head, she tried to shift away from him but even that caused the friction to drive her higher.

Harrison saw the look and knew exactly what she was trying to do. He didn't understand why, because what she was doing to them felt...perfect! Incredible!

And then he remembered her innocence. She'd never done this before, she had no idea how to handle this part of her sexuality. "Ah, love, just go with it," he urged. He shifted his body slightly, showing her what could happen.

"No!" she snapped at him but her body arched and he moved deeper. "No no no!" she screamed, but her hands whipped down to his hips, pulling him in and her own hips shifted, trying to take him deeper into her body.

"Do you still want me to stop?" he teased.

"No!" she gasped. "Don't you dare stop!" and then screamed, arching her back when he pulled almost all the way out of her heat and then slammed back into her. "Again!" she demanded. And of course, he gave in to that demand. But then things turned crazy and he was no longer smiling. She just felt too perfect and, no matter how hard he tried, he couldn't slow down. She pulled him in, urging him faster and he was more than happy to comply.

All too quickly, he felt her body start to splinter apart into her second climax and he watched in fascination as she screamed, her nails digging into his shoulders as the waves of pleasure washed over her. And just that quickly, he was coming to his own orgasm. It was the most intense moment of his life and he couldn't hold back. He tried to slow down, to make it last longer for her but his body was in control and the only thing he could do was to keep himself from falling on top of her. He didn't want to crush her with his weight so when he was finally able to breathe, he rolled over, pulling her next to him as they both gasped for breath.

A long time later, he felt her move. Glancing down at her, he realized that she was trying to pull the covers over her. "Are you cold?" he asked, rolling so that he was over her once again but he held his weight off of her with his arms.

Sierra stared up at him, still shocked by what had just happened. Was she cold? With his muscular body next to hers? Was that even possible?

She opened her mouth to tell him yes because she wanted to hide, to bury her face in a pillow and pretend that he had not just done such amazingly naughty things to her body.

"No," she finally whispered honestly, her fingers still clutching the comforter even if she didn't pull it closer.

His eyes looked at her fingers fisting on the material, then down at her eyes. "So why are you trying to cover yourself?" he asked softly. He shifted so that his weight was on one side, freeing up one of his hands. His fingers moved to her waist, testing the skin and noting how soft she was.

Sierra's heart rate instantly picked up and she grabbed his hand.

"Ah," he thought and chuckled. "You don't want to do that again," he surmised. "Care to explain to me how a woman of your age and beauty was still a virgin?" he asked, his eyes moving down her naked body, enjoying the way her nipples hardened and he hadn't even touched them.

"No," Sierra replied, but she wasn't sure if she was telling him no for the question or no for his head that was slowly lowering. She knew what he was going to do and she shook her head, trying to scoot away.

Harrison only laughed when presented with her back but his hands took control of her hips. "If you're going to deny me your breasts, then your back is just as effective," he told her. His hands then slid across her back, exactly where he'd discovered she was sensitive earlier.

Sierra couldn't believe what was happening to her. Once again, his touch was driving her wild. She wasn't even facing him and she still couldn't pull back. When his hand pushed her leg forward, she was already lost in that sensual haze that he could put her into. So when he slowly thrust into her body, she was shocked. Her head went back and her body arched, trying to give him more room. And just as before, he took her higher and higher, those sensations driving her wild until the stars burst around her and she was clenching the comforter in her hands while the waves of pleasure washed over her. She wasn't even aware of his own orgasm which quickly followed her own. All she knew afterwards was how gentle he was as he pulled her into his arms while she fell asleep, feeling more secure than she had in years.

Chapter 5

Sierra fiddled with the button on her blouse, unable to look at Harrison as the plane taxied to a stop. They were on some tropical island in the Caribbean and she was nervous about what was to come. Over and over last night, he'd made love to her, only to have her collapse into his arms and fall back to sleep.

She didn't like losing control, she thought as the airport staff rushed out of the terminal to push a staircase up to the private plane.

"Are you ready?" Harrison asked, standing up and offering her his hand.

"Ready?" she asked, her mind still stuck on last night's insanity and wondering how she could stop that from happening again. But did she really want that to stop?

Of course she did! She wasn't like that! And she didn't like this man! She barely knew him!

Harrison waited patiently for Sierra to take his hand. The doors to the plane opened up and still he waited, wondering what was going through her mind. In the end, she sighed and put her small, delicate hand into his larger one and he closed his fingers around hers, helping her out of the seat. But he didn't release her hand, keeping her close even while they descended the stairs. A jeep was waiting at the bottom of the stairs, one of the other staff members already loading up the back with their luggage into the old, dilapidated vehicle that was invented before Ford took over making the modern day Jeep. Fortunately, this vehicle ran as if it had only been created yesterday!

He noticed that Sierra only had one bag and thought that was odd. But he would fix that, he thought. He'd take her shopping and dress her up, filling up more bags to take home. He wanted to shower her with gifts, which was a strange notion. He was used to women teasing and cajoling him to buy them things but this little woman wasn't doing any of those tricks and he respected her more because of that.

"What's on your mind?" he asked as he led her down the staircase.

Sierra sighed, pushing her hair out of her eyes as the wind whipped it out of place. "I'm fine," she lied, wishing she had the courage to talk to him. But he scared her. The man could do things to her, make her want things…make her want him!

He led her over to the passenger side of the jeep and closed the door with her in the passenger seat. Since the top was off, he could still talk to her. "You're not fine. Something is on your mind. Are you going to talk to me?"

Sierra looked down at her hands, her fingers twisting in her lap. "I'm fine," she repeated, nervous now because he had that hard look in his blue eyes.

Harrison sighed. "Fine. But we have two weeks here on the island. Eventually, you're going to learn to trust me and you'll explain what's going on in that lovely head of yours." With that, he tapped the metal door before walking to the driver's side. He pulled himself in and drove out of the airport. It took twenty minutes, but the drive along the coast of Grand Cayman was exhilarating. He could feel her starting to relax as the warmth of the Caribbean sun beat down on them. She laughed as the wind whipped her hair around and his body reacted to the erotic sound. She was such a sensuous being, why was she shying away from him now? They'd spent an incredible night in bed together and she had to know that they would be spending two whole weeks in naked glory with each other.

But she was still a mystery. He was going to get to the bottom of whatever was bothering her, one way or another. And he also knew that he was going to enjoy the adventure too.

When he pulled up in front of a white, stone building, Sierra simply sat there and stared, too anxious about what was going to happen when she went inside that lovely house.

"What's wrong?" Harrison asked, leaning an arm along the steering wheel so he could look down at her.

"This is your vacation home?" she asked, her voice barely above a whisper. She was staring at the house with enormous eyes, trying to digest and accept what was coming next.

"Yes. One of them. Is that a problem?"

She turned her head as she sighed. "I suppose not." She looked at him for a long moment. "You're going to want to make love again, aren't you?"

Harrison couldn't stop the laughter at her question. It was such a crazy question and he would have thought, after last night, that the answer was obvious. "Absolutely."

"Because you need an heir."

He picked up a lock of her hair that was now tousled from the wind. "No. I don't want to make love to you because I need an heir. I want to make love to you because I thoroughly enjoyed last night." He watched her eyes soften before he said, "You did too, didn't you?" He knew that she had. But he wanted to see if she would admit it.

Sierra opened her mouth to deny him but the only word that came out was, "Yes."

"So why are you suddenly nervous about sharing a bed for the next two weeks with me?"

She turned her head as she tried to work through the issues that weren't all that clear in her mind. "Well, perhaps because we don't really know each other. We're married," she said, but shrugged her shoulders. "We're married but we don't know very much about each other. And that just feels…wrong."

His finger twirled her hair around his finger, enjoying the softness. "Did it feel wrong last night?"

She considered her words carefully and he stopped her.

"I'm not talking about what you felt afterwards. I'm asking if my touch felt wrong. If I did something that you didn't like?"

She had to be honest with him. Looking up into his midnight blue eyes, she shook her head. "No."

"But afterwards, you felt wrong."

She couldn't look at him any longer. Staring through the windshield, she admitted, "I felt ashamed. We've spent so little time in each other's company."

"Let me get this straight. You were ashamed because someone else has dictated how long you should know a man before you are allowed to enjoy being intimate with him. Is that what you're trying to say?"

She thought about it and realized that, yes, he was right on the mark. "I guess that seems a bit silly when you put it that way."

His lips quirked up slightly. "It isn't silly if it makes you feel ashamed. I'm not asking you to feel any specific way, Sierra."

"But when we enter that house…"

He chuckled. "Yes. I'm going to make love to you."

"Because you need an heir."

He shook his head. "No. I'm going to make love to you because I honestly don't think I could keep my hands off of you. You're beautiful and intelligent, gentle and caring. And I disagree with your opinion on how long two people should know each other before they have sex, but I'm not going to disregard your feelings either."

"So we can hold off on sex?"

He laughed. "How about this, we'll go inside, I'll open a bottle of wine and we'll see what my housekeeper has prepared for dinner. And if you don't want to have sex tonight, we won't."

She waited, wondering what conditions he might put on that statement. But when he remained silent, she looked back at him. "That's it? If I don't want to have sex, we won't?"

He shrugged. "I'm still going to do everything I can to change your mind and help you feel more comfortable. It's our honeymoon, after all."

She wasn't sure she liked the sound of that.

"I'll also do everything I can to make you reach the point where you're more comfortable. And you have to sleep next to me."

She swallowed, thinking that might be the hard part.

"You're getting the picture, aren't you?" He leaned down and kissed her, loving the way her lips instantly softened as she kissed him back. She might have some odd ideas about knowing someone for a long period of time before becoming intimate, but she couldn't resist the pull of their attraction any more than he could.

When he felt the need to pull her onto his lap and make love to her in the jeep, he pulled away, looking down into her silver eyes. "How about that bottle of wine and conversation?" he suggested.

Sierra looked at him and wanted to pull his mouth back to hers. Goodness, she loved kissing him. And touching him. And all that other stuff that she shouldn't like. But she admitted, at least to herself, that she really did.

"Wine sounds good," she finally replied.

A black eyebrow went up in amusement. "But not the conversation?" he teased.

She smiled, feeling more relaxed now. "Conversation would be very nice."

She stepped out of the jeep and moved to the back but he only took her hand and shook his head. "The staff will get the suitcases out and bring them to our room. Let's have a drink." He led her up the steps and into a beautiful house decorated in cool, white tiles but with splashes of color, all set against the backdrop of the ocean that sparkled as the sun slowly lowered to the horizon.

"It's beautiful," she sighed as he handed her a glass of wine.

"To us," he said and clinked her glass with his.

She sipped the wine and looked over the rim of the glass at him, wondering what he was thinking. But he was very good at not revealing anything he didn't want someone to see.

True to his word though, they ate a delicious fish dinner out on the patio while the waves crashed against the shoreline. And they talked! They discussed all kinds of topics and she smiled, laughed, found herself arguing with him and agreeing with him. He was funny and insightful and Sierra was amazed by the depth of his knowledge.

By the time the night had fallen over the island, Sierra's nervousness was completely gone. Perhaps it was the wine, or maybe it was his conversation or even the lack of pressure. But when he pulled her up out of the chair where she'd been curled up, she willingly went into his arms. They spent the next several hours exploring each other's bodies, finding out what each liked the most and talking in between lovemaking. To Sierra, it was the most incredible night of her life.

Over the next two weeks, she learned more about the man who was her husband as well as visited extraordinary tropical sites and loved every moment of it. Harrison took her to the sea turtle farm and Sierra got to hold a baby sea turtle. She loved the little guys and was amazed at how fast they were. The butterfly farm was magical, snorkeling along the shore was stunning and she laughed and screamed when Harrison took her out to Sting Ray City, a sand dune way out in the ocean where dozens of enormous stingrays swarmed around visitors. He even showed her how to feed the enormous sea creatures, then caught her when she screamed and jumped into his arms when their mouths freaked her out. Their mouths were like a vacuum cleaner sucking up the squid in her hand and her only reaction was to jump up to him for protection. He laughed the whole time, enjoying the way she felt and her reactions.

All the time in between, he was either making love to her or he allowed her to question him about his life and his preferences. In return, she reciprocated and answered all of his questions, even allowed him to interrogate her about the time when her father was arrested. Some of his questions didn't make any sense but they all brought back memories, both painful and happy.

When they finally boarded a plane back to London, she admitted that she was sad to be leaving the island.

"We'll come back," he promised, kissing the top of her head as they stepped up the stairs to board his private plane.

Chapter 6

Sierra smiled as she stepped out of the limousine. She hated traveling like this, but Harrison insisted on it. And for some reason, she wanted to make him happy.

He'd certainly been kind enough to her.

She stopped walking part way to the building. Kind? No, Harrison was not kind. He was wonderful, annoying, generous and obnoxious, opinionated and intelligent. But he was not kind. Never could anyone ever describe him as kind. Overly protective? Absolutely. But not kind.

She actually laughed at the idea and thought about telling him that he was kind, just to see the reaction on his face. She would love to see it. He would be so irritated and he might just...she laughed, thinking about what he might do. And shivered, excited by all of the possibilities.

She also had no idea why Harrison had insisted on her meeting him here for lunch. They'd spent the last two weeks together. But she wasn't going to argue with him. She'd finished cleaning the stalls and helping Bob with some of the other chores around the stables this morning so it was nice to get back into a routine and see her horses again, but she was actually excited to see Harrison. Perhaps she'd just gotten used to his demanding presence during their honeymoon and not being around him was...boring.

As she rode up in the elevator, she smoothed down the skirt she'd chosen for today's lunch, wondering if Harrison would like it. He was always so complimentary about her outfits and she liked trying to anticipate what he might like.

With a sigh, she pushed all of those frivolous thoughts out of her mind. She was here for lunch with her temporary husband, nothing more. And the only reason she wanted to please him was because he'd been so generous towards her since he'd stepped back into her life. Never had he implied that she was promiscuous. He'd never brought up the fact that she'd kissed him during her engagement party to another man. In fact, he was always extremely polite.

Except in bed.

No, he wasn't polite in bed at all! The opposite of polite, she thought. Her eyes almost rolled into the back of her head as she remembered all of the pleasure his impoliteness had given her over the past few weeks. Even this morning…

The doors to the elevator opened up and she stepped out, taking a deep breath to try and control her rampant thoughts. It was completely inappropriate to…

Harrison stepped out of his office, his blue eyes slashing across the expanse as she walked forward. The heat in those eyes stopped her cold. She couldn't take another step, could barely even breathe.

He walked over to her and took her hand, leading her into his office. "You look beautiful," he told her as he closed the doors to his office.

Sierra's mind was mush. She knew that look. She knew what he was thinking and it made her stomach muscles tighten. It made everything inside of her tighten! She wasn't even aware of her mouth falling open but he noticed and he pulled her closer.

"Damn, you're beautiful," he growled as he covered her mouth with his.

A long time later, he lifted his head. "I'd better stop before we're both unable to."

Sierra was pretty sure that she was already to that point but she bowed her head, thinking that she was becoming a bit too voracious when he was around.

"Let's go to lunch," he said and took her hand, leading her out of his office. "Tell me what you have been doing this morning."

She happily walked beside him, feeling strange now that they were back in the real world. She thought about how casual they'd been with each other in the Caribbean but it felt strange to act the same way here in London. It was almost as if they were different people, she thought.

But as she looked up into his eyes, she wondered why that had to be. Before coming back, she would have leaned into him and he would wrap his arms around her when she'd done that. So instead of standing on the opposite side of the elevator, she walked closer and pressed her shoulder against his. Instantly, his arm moved around her shoulder, pulling her closer to him and she felt her heart melt a bit more towards this man.

With a bright smile, she watched the numbers indicating that they were descending. "I've been helping Bob in the stables," she told him, looking up at the numbers over the doors instead of at him. There were a few other people in the elevator with them now, although they all recognized him and gave him much more space than any other person might receive while riding in the elevators.

The doors opened and Harrison took her hand, leading her through the lobby and the two of them were automatically surrounded by his bodyguards once again. She hurried to keep up with his longer stride but she also knew that he was trying to get her into the limousine quickly. Yet another protective measure from him.

When they sat down at the restaurant, he whipped his napkin open. "I don't want you working in the stables any longer, Sierra," he told her firmly. He nodded to the waiter who was standing by with a bottle of white wine.

Sierra's mouth fell open. "Not work? But…"

He shook his head and she waited until the waiter had poured the wine and departed. "Go to school full time. Register for more classes or do whatever you want to do, but you're not working any longer."

She looked at the wine glass now filled with what she suspected was a very expensive vintage. Sierra wasn't really sure how to respond to that. "Harrison, I want to work."

"No. Absolutely not. You have been working in the stables for too long. It isn't the job for you."

She took a deep breath, trying to calm down her anger. "You can't stop me from working."

He chuckled. "Sierra, would you like to reconsider that argument?"

She flushed. "Of course. I'm working in your stables and you can fire me if you'd like." She looked down at the menu but her eyes didn't see the descriptions of the options. She only saw his hard, blue eyes that were telling her to stop doing something she loved. "But I'm asking you not to."

"It is done. You can consider yourself resigned or fired, whichever makes you feel better, but you're not working in the stables any longer." His eyes fired up as he looked across the table at her. "Hopefully, you'll be pregnant soon, if you aren't already, and it will be a moot point anyway."

Sierra's hand fluttered to her stomach and she suddenly felt cold. Of course, he wanted her to be pregnant. He had to produce an heir in order to hold onto his title. That's all she was to him.

Silly her, she thought as she sipped the ice water. She'd been walking around in a happy daze, thinking that she missed him when all he wanted was to create an heir so that he could continue on with his privileged existence.

That wasn't really fair, she thought. Harrison worked hard. He'd been up before her every morning during their honeymoon, making phone calls and doing something on his computer. He was not one of those weak aristocrats who lived off of rents. He was smart and applied himself, worked very hard and had high standards for the people that worked for him.

But still…

She was hurt that he thought of her only as a womb that would ensure his title. But that's all he'd promised her going into this relationship. She was the only one in this relationship that had gone further. She's the one that had let her emotions get involved.

"Right," she replied. "So what's today's lunch agenda?" she asked, fiddling with her knife and fork.

Harrison noticed the strange note to her voice and looked up from perusing the menu. "Are you okay?" he asked carefully.

Sierra met his glance, refusing to believe that there was any sort of concern in those blue eyes. She'd believed that he was a kinder person before and now she was struggling to pull herself back from that fallacy.

"I'm fine. But I enjoy working in the stables."

"Not going to happen, Sierra. You can ride the horses all you want, at least until you conceive, but no working. Have Bob hire someone else to help him out in the stables. But you are no longer allowed to even saddle your horse."

She bit her tongue with that command. There was no way she was going to adhere to that edict. She loved saddling her mare, brushing her down and making sure she had food, water and hay. It was a bonding time for her and her spritely companion who had gotten her through some of the roughest periods in her life.

"I won't muck out the stalls anymore," she promised. Sort of, she silently added. She was still going down to the stables, was still going to do what she wanted to do. She loved the horses, loved all the animals. And she wasn't going to let this arrogant man tell her that she couldn't take care of them. All of those tender, warm-hearted feelings she'd been having as she'd walked into his building earlier to meet him were banished because of his harsh and uncompromising edict.

"Anything else?" she asked, pulling back when the waiter arrived with her salad. She noticed that Harrison had ordered salmon and she stopped herself from wrinkling up her nose. She had always hated salmon. It was more than a little creepy to be eating the pink meat. She didn't understand why because she enjoyed other kinds of seafood and loved a good steak, although she hadn't been able to afford it recently.

"You don't like salmon," he said.

Sierra looked up, startled that she'd been so transparent.

"Salmon is fine," she lied.

Harrison chuckled. "You obviously hate it. Why would you try and pretend otherwise?"

She shrugged. "Just trying to be polite," she replied.

An hour later, Harrison walked her back to his office. He'd questioned her about her day's plans and encouraged her to visit a spa. Sierra agreed, but she secretly hated the idea. She used to spend a great deal of time at spas and salons, getting her nails and hair done. It seemed like a complete waste of time and money now. She'd learned that there were so many more interesting things to do.

"I have something for you," he said as he led her into his office. He took an envelope out of his top drawer and handed it to her. "Here are credit cards and bank account information. Feel free to spend whatever you need."

Where was the sweet, caring man she'd spent so much time with in Grand Cayman? Where was the man who made her laugh, challenged her opinions and listened to her talk? This man was hard and rude and just as arrogant as she remembered him. She felt awkward taking the envelope and wanted to reject it. "I don't think…"

"Take the credit cards, Sierra. There's a gala tomorrow night. Can you be ready? It is formal."

Sierra cringed, wishing she could say no to that. But she was his wife now. "I will be ready," she said, straightening her shoulders as if she had to brace herself for the event.

"Good. Roger will drive you home. I'll see you later." He leaned in and kissed her, sending those telling ripples throughout her body once again.

Instead of lifting her head up for more, she turned and walked out of his office, not wanting to make a fool of herself once again. Once a day was enough, she thought firmly.

She needed to focus on what was important – finding Daniel and getting back to school, into a routine. Daniel had to be her top priority, but she wasn't sure how to locate him when he didn't want to be found. Besides, he was nineteen years old, an adult now. If he wanted to disappear, there really wasn't anything she could do to stop him. She'd left him several messages and she'd received one back from him, telling her that he was okay but was "trying to get things straight". What that entailed, she had no idea, nor would he call her to explain.

So she was going to give him his space, let him work out whatever it was he was working out. She also suspected that Harrison knew where he was. She might be hurt right now, but she trusted him to tell her if something had happened to Daniel.

She was halfway across the wide courtyard when she heard her name called out. Looking up, she spotted Patrick, her father's former business partner, hurrying across the courtyard towards her.

He stopped in front of her, a bit too close for her peace of mind and she had to step backwards. "Patrick!" she greeted him, surprised by the eager expression on his features. "How nice to see you," she lied, falling back into the old rules and social niceties her mother had taught her.

The last time she'd seen him he'd looked like he'd rather scrape poop off of his shoe with his fingernails before speaking politely to her. He hadn't even bothered to attend Sierra's father's funeral, but then again, why would he? Her father had supposedly stolen money from this man as well.

Even after all this time, she still had a hard time believing that of her father. While they'd been on their honeymoon, Harrison had asked her several questions about her father's investments before he'd been arrested and some of her answers were coming back to mind. It suddenly occurred to her that this man might know a bit more about what had happened back then. If only she could get him to consider the possibility that her father might be innocent, perhaps Patrick could help her investigate the embezzlement. But it had occurred so long ago, was there even an evidence trail to follow? Or had three years obliterated the evidence?

"What can I do for you, Patrick?" she asked as politely as possible, ideas spinning through her mind.

"How have you been?" he asked, looking at her with a smug expression on his features. "I heard you married well. A good way to get out of the muck from your previous life, eh?"

His words were offensive and condescending, shocking her as she looked at the man who had been good friends with her father. She suddenly realized that she truly hated this man. He was disgusting and his innuendos were completely inappropriate. This had been her father's friend and business partner, but at the first sign of trouble, he'd thrown her father under the bus, accusing him of all sorts of improprieties. The police couldn't have gotten very far without this man's help. That realization hit her hard, and it angered her. Not to mention, his question was tasteless and crass. "Was there a question?" she asked sharply.

Patrick's smile faltered slightly but he rallied. "I know you're probably still reeling from your father's crimes all those years ago, but I wanted you to know that I don't have any hard feelings. It was your father who committed the grievous actions against our clients. Not you or Daniel."

Sierra stood there, not able to speak.

Patrick continued on awkwardly. "How is Daniel doing these days? He came to my office right after...well, after your father's arrest."

This was news. Daniel hadn't mentioned a visit to her father's old office. "What did he want?"

"A job," Patrick replied. "He was asking for a job." Patrick shook his head as if that were a ludicrous idea. "The kid has balls, I'll give him that."

Sierra was stunned. Why hadn't Daniel mentioned that to her? He'd been so distant. And she still hadn't been able to reach him since he'd stormed out after their harsh words with each other. He'd been completely under the radar and he hadn't returned any of her phone calls or text messages.

But Patrick's announcement was astounding. "So you blame Daniel for our father's crimes but not me?" she clarified, becoming more offended the longer the disgusting man spoke.

Elizabeth Lennox

Patrick stammered for a moment. "Of course not," he backtracked. "Absolutely not. But you know…it was Daniel! I mean… what was I supposed to do?"

Sierra shrugged her shoulders. "I don't know. Perhaps believe in my father's innocence. You were business partners for decades. Was there any evidence of embezzlement before my father's arrest?" she asked.

"Of course not!"

"So it was only my father. And only one instance of a crime."

Patrick opened and closed his mouth. "Well, that's all we know about. That one instance."

She stared at him, more pieces of the puzzle starting to come into focus. They didn't fit into the overall picture, but there was more that she didn't understand. "So your accounting personnel didn't do a thorough scrub of the books to ensure that there were no other instances of crimes or embezzlement? Isn't that odd?" Everything the man was saying made her more curious to find out the truth. Before, she'd been too stunned to look into the matter. And the bad news just kept getting worse, then her parents died and it was all she could do to get out of bed each morning.

But now, looking at the man, her mind was spinning with all of the un-answered questions. This time around, she had the backing of the powerful Duke of Selton to help her, she suddenly realized.

"Of course we did a thorough search through all the files."

"And didn't find anything wrong?"

"Not that we could find," Patrick responded but there was a look in his eyes that Sierra didn't trust.

She didn't say anything more. She was going to have to discuss this with Harrison tonight. She still wasn't convinced. Something was definitely wrong here.

Patrick smiled and Sierra remembered that cheesy smile from the last time he'd been at her house. It instantly made her skin crawl.

"Listen, Sierra. This is all water under the bridge. Hey, my daughter is selling cookies for a fundraiser for her school. Any chance you'd like to buy some? I can guarantee that they are delicious!"

Sierra thought about just brushing off the guy but she wasn't sure she could get to the limousine fast enough. "Fine," she replied. "How much are they?" she asked, digging into her purse and pulling out her wallet.

"They're only three pounds a box," he told her.

Sierra wondered why a man with the kind of wealth Patrick claimed to have would let his daughter sell cookies for three pounds a box. It didn't make sense. Didn't these types just write a check and let their kids off the hook for selling stuff?

70

Unfortunately, her wallet was empty. "I don't have any cash on me right now," she explained, remembering that she'd used the last of her cash to buy a bagel this morning.

"You can write a check," he told her hopefully, his eyes glancing down at the depths of her purse where the envelope containing checks and credit cards rested. Sierra had forgotten that Harrison had mentioned bank information after lunch and she stared at the envelope warily.

Sierra was just about to tell him that she didn't have any checks. She hadn't had a bank balance that could hold any money in it after she paid her bills, so there hadn't ever been a reason to carry a checkbook.

She opened the envelope and found the credit cards and a checkbook, pulling it out. "Here's a pen," Patrick said smoothly, handing her a pen she knew cost around two hundred pounds that he had in his pocket.

Sierra remembered that Evan had bragged about pens like this while they were dating and, at the time, she'd thought that it seemed silly to spend so much money on a pen. Did it really write so much better than a pen from the office supply store that cost merely two or three pounds? She doubted it.

Shrugging, she wrote out a check for fifteen pounds, not sure what she was going to do with five boxes of cookies, but hey, she could give them to Daniel. If she could find him!

"Here you go," she told him.

He took the check and slipped it into his pocket. "I'll send the cookies to Harrison's office. They'll be there by tomorrow."

A moment later, she was watching his back retreat from her view and wondering why he'd looked so smug. The man was strange and creepy, she thought. Why hadn't she seen that when she was younger? Why had her father put so much faith in the man?

Or had he not been this smug three years ago?

She stepped into the limousine, her mind spinning with the information she'd just heard. Something wasn't right. She just knew it!

Chapter 7

Sierra took the glass of champagne but she didn't really want it. She wanted to go home, curl up with Harrison and read a good book. Or talk with him. Or even better, have him touch her like he had the other night.

"What are you thinking?" he asked as he stepped closer to her, his broad shoulder suddenly blocking out the rest of the room.

Sierra felt her face warm up even more but she smiled up at him. "Nothing at all," she lied. She'd promised herself that she was going to be cool about her relationship with Harrison. She couldn't let her feelings become involved. Or, more specifically, she couldn't allow her feelings to become more involved than they already were.

Harrison could tell that her mind had gone off in another direction and he wanted details. "Remember the last time you wouldn't tell me something?" he asked, his fingers tangling with her free hand.

Sierra's breath caught in her throat and she clenched the champagne flute more tightly. "Yes," she whispered.

"Think you can hold out longer this time around?" he asked her, moving even closer to her. They were so close, she could feel his pants leg moving against her skirt.

"No," she told him, holding eye contact with him for as long as possible. Gone was all of her anger and resentment at his "no-working" dictate. On the drive home from his office yesterday, she'd come to the conclusion that she could do whatever she wanted, he didn't have to pay her. She could still help Bob down at the stables and if he ever found out, she could deal with his anger then. Until that point, she would continue to do what she loved.

She also tried to discuss the issue of her father's crimes with him, but he had closed down, telling her to drop it. She hadn't understood, but she'd attributed his attitude to his protectiveness.

None of that mattered right now. All she knew was that she wanted this man with an urgency that she couldn't believe, but couldn't suppress either.

"Good," he chuckled. He put his arm around her waist, pulling her closer. "I like that about you," he told her softly.

Sierra smiled, secretly thrilled that he could read her so easily. And he ignited all of her synapses to fire up, making her think about things she hadn't ever considered about herself before. "When can we leave?" she asked, leaning against him slightly, showing him without words that she wanted him. How brazen of her, she thought as she shifted slightly, loving the hard angles of his arm underneath the staid material of his tuxedo.

"Right now! Let's go," he told her.

She immediately turned around, enjoying the way his hand stayed on the small of her back, telling her that he was just as intent on leaving as she was.

Sierra almost groaned out loud when she spotted the man coming towards them. Evan. Her ex-fiancée.

"Isn't that…" Harrison asked.

"Yes," Sierra replied before he even needed to finish his sentence. "Can we…"

"Sierra!" Evan called out, lifting his glass of scotch into the air. His voice was so loud that several people turned to glare at him for his rudeness. "You're even more beautiful now than you were three years ago. How the hell are you?"

Sierra leaned in closer to Harrison when it looked like Evan was going to kiss her. "I'm fine," she replied to the man who had gained about thirty pounds over the years. He hadn't been very old, just out of university when they'd been dating. So he was only in his mid to late twenties but the years had not been kind to him. His weight gain had caused his cheeks to bloat out and his hair was already receding, something that most men were able to avoid until they reached their late thirties. "How are you?" She didn't really care though.

Evan chuckled. "I'm great!" and he spread his arms out as if to indicate that his "greatness" was obvious. "You did well for yourself," and he sloshed his glass up towards Harrison. Looking up at the taller man, he said, "Want to come back to our firm? I know that you had problems in the past," and he not-so-subtly looked at Sierra again, "but we've built up our reputation again and we're rock solid."

Sierra's eyes narrowed and she felt the hairs on the back of her neck stand up. She moved even closer to Harrison, putting her hand on his flat stomach as if she needed to somehow protect him. "I spoke to Patrick yesterday and he mentioned that you've audited the accounts. Are you sure that the accountants didn't find anything out of the ordinary?" She felt Harrison stiffen and remembered how he'd warned her to leave it alone.

But she wasn't going to leave it. This was too important so Sierra watched carefully and…right there! A flash! Evan's eyes clouded over for a moment! Something wasn't right! She could just feel it in her bones.

"Of course our accountants went through everything. They're very careful."

Sierra noticed that he didn't elaborate. It was almost as if he knew that the measures taken weren't adequate. She was more sure now than ever that something wasn't right. Her father hadn't done the embezzling! Something smelled rotten!

How could she prove it though? What could she do to find out the truth?

She felt Harrison's thumb move across a spot on her back and somehow, that movement reassured her. "Sorry Evan, but we were just on our way out," Harrison was saying.

He looked surprised. "But the night is still young. Have a drink and let's talk about…"

"We're on our way to another event," Harrison interrupted, placing a hand on her back and gently moved her forward.

Evan was not to be deterred. "How about if I call your office to set up a meeting?" he offered hopefully.

Harrison nodded his head and, for a moment, Sierra thought he was actually considering the possibility of investing money with the firm. But he said instead, "Contact my assistant. She'll see if there is an opening in my schedule." And with that, they moved through crowds that were, thankfully, too deep for Evan to follow them.

Sierra kept her mouth shut until they were in the privacy of his limousine but as soon as the doors were closed and the privacy window shut, she turned to face him. "I need your help."

Harrison looked down at her and instantly knew what she wanted from him. "I'm not sure if I can, Sierra."

She wasn't going to accept that. And she shouldn't have years ago. "My father didn't steal that money," she said forcefully. "And I know there are ways to prove that. At the time, I didn't have the mental capacity to deal with all of the problems coming at me, but now I'd like to clear his name. I'd like to figure out what really happened and make it right."

Harrison shook his head. "Your father is dead, Sierra. And your brother might be okay for the moment, but his temper is still out of control. Why not focus on the future, trying to get your brother's head on straight?"

She huffed angrily as she sat back on the seat. "Because my brother isn't returning my calls. I have no idea where he is and I haven't seen him since the day he…" she looked up at his handsome features and grimaced. "Well, since the day he brought home all of the stuff he stole from you."

Harrison took her hand. "Let me help with your brother. That's something that would be more productive than trying to figure out what happened with your father."

She bit her lip, trying not to get angry with him. "Daniel is my responsibility. But I don't have the power to do anything to re-open the investigation into my father's criminal accusations. He didn't get a trial because the heart attack killed him almost right after he was arrested. So he had no way to clear his name."

"The evidence against him was pretty overwhelming, Sierra. I looked into it three years ago."

She looked up at him hopefully. "You did?" She faced him once again. "Why did you do that?" Her heart was pounding in her chest and she ached to hear the words that he'd investigated because he'd felt something that night, that he hadn't believed that her father would do something and he wanted to help her.

"Because I don't allow anyone to mess with my money or my companies," he told her softly but with a force in his voice that told her so much.

With those words, her wounded heart plummeted once again. She turned her head to look out the window, fighting to hide the hurt. She'd wanted so badly for him to express some feelings towards her, give her some indication that she meant more to him than just...than just a womb.

When was she going to learn? When was she going to stop hoping for anything more? She was such a fool.

"I understand," she told him. But already, her mind was shifting, trying to figure things out for herself. If Harrison wasn't going to help her, surely there was a way to do this on her own.

It suddenly occurred to her that Harrison gave her an enormous allowance each month. Why couldn't she use that to hire an investigator? Why was she relying on someone else to get something done? All she really needed was the money and she could start to investigate herself!

"What are you thinking, Sierra?" he asked, pulling her hand back onto his lap. She felt his hard thigh on the back of her hand and tried very hard to suppress the shiver of awareness. She didn't want to feel this for him. She wanted to be as heartless towards him as he was being towards her. This was a business relationship as he'd so blithely pointed out. She was here to help him retain his title and he was going to help her with school which would eventually help her become independent.

"You're mad at me." Harrison looked down at her with amusement. He actually chuckled when she turned her head back to glare up at him. "Why are you mad?"

"It's nothing," she said, trying to wave away her hurt and anger. She would let her determination push aside everything else. If he wanted to be self-centered, then so could she, she told herself. She would focus her energy on getting her degree, trying to find Daniel and get him into school and then prove her father's innocence. Harrison had set the terms of their marriage. It was now time she started to follow them as well and stop thinking that...stop thinking that there was more to their relationship.

"It is obviously something," he argued, lifting her up and settling her back down onto his lap. "Tell me what you are thinking."

She pulled back but his hands on her hips wouldn't let her move too far away. "No."

His eyebrows went up with her adamant reply. "No?" he repeated, thinking he'd never heard her say that word to him. Well, except on their wedding night when she'd been too nervous. What worked once would probably work again, he thought.

"Ah, you're going to challenge me, eh?"

She shook her head quickly, realizing what he was about to do. "No Harrison. My thoughts are private."

Her lips were compressed into a tight little rosebud pout and her silver eyes narrowed with intent. All of it was turning him on. Gone was his need to know what she was thinking and crashing all around him was the need to hold her, to feel her body under his own. His hands slid up her waist and he ignored her when her hands tried to grab his wrists. "What else is private?" he asked, his eyes moving down to her breasts and, instantly, Sierra felt her nipples tighten in response.

She tugged ineffectively at his wrists, wanting to stop him but he was relentless. "No. I'm mad at you. We're not having sex tonight." Not to mention, his hands felt incredible on her body!

He laughed softly. "Okay. If you don't want to have sex, that's fine with me. Just say no."

A fraction of a second later, his thumb tweaked her nipple and she gasped, her hands clenching his wrists for a whole different reason now. "Harrison," she moaned, her eyes closing and she lost her will to resist him. That easily, he could overcome her objections to the point where she wanted him so badly, she didn't care where they were.

He shifted her so that her legs were straddling him. "Tell me what you were thinking," he commanded, his thumb flicking over her nipple again.

She shook her head. "Do that again, please," she begged, leaning forward to try and put her breast in the way of his errant thumbs. "Please," she cried softly.

"Tell me what you were thinking, Sierra," he said and leaned forward, taking her nipple in his mouth through the soft fabric of her dress.

She shook her head, biting her lower lip to try and control any admission that might explode from her desperate need for his touch.

When his fingers moved away from her breast, her eyes snapped open. "What are you doing?" she demanded.

"Tell me," he ordered once again.

Sierra stared at him, furious that he would be so brutal in his desire to know her thoughts. He knew her body thoroughly, but he was forgetting that she had gotten to know his body as well. She knew all of the ways to drive him just as crazy.

Harrison saw the smile start to form on her beautiful features and, in a second, he knew that he was in trouble. She pushed back on his lap and fell to the seat next to him. When her fingers fell to his legs, he groaned, loving the feeling of her soft fingers against his body. She so rarely touched him of her own volition so this was an extra treat.

But then her fingers moved higher. When he felt her fingers on his zipper, he almost shot out of the seat. He grabbed her hands, but by that point, her adept fingers had already grabbed him, wrapping those incredible fingers around his erection. After that, he was hers and there was no way he would, could, stop her. When she took him into her warm, hot mouth, his head slammed back against the leather seats and he couldn't do anything other than let his fingers slide through her soft, thick hair while she tortured him with her mouth and hands.

When the limousine pulled up outside of his house, he lifted her into his arms and adjusted his clothing quickly. By the time his chauffer opened the door, he already had Sierra's hands in his. He couldn't even wait for her to step out of the vehicle. Instead, he lifted her into his arms and carried her inside, slamming the front door closed behind him.

"Now!" he told her, lifting her up and pressing her back against the wall.

Sierra smiled when he made that command, feeling exhilarated as he lifted her higher and she wrapped her legs around his hips. A split second later, the scrap of black lace she'd worn earlier was torn from her body and Harrison's fingers slid easily into her heat. She gasped as his fingers tortured her flesh, moving in and out, pressing against all of the sensitive areas and making her scream with her need. Only then did he shift and slide himself into her, filling her up so perfectly.

With the wall against her back and his hands under her bottom, he lifted her once more and started moving, sliding in and out of her. The incredible feel of him like this made her scream and she could barely control her climax as he pulled her into the vortex, not allowing her to hold back in any way. She was powerless as the waves crashed over her again and again. All she could do was hold onto his broad shoulders and ride out the pleasure until she felt him climax as well.

There was a long silence while he continued to hold her there against the wall. She felt his body relax but he still didn't lift his head from her neck.

"I'm sorry," he growled, his hands trying to soothe her body. "That was rude of me."

Sierra slowly released the fists of hair on his head that she'd unknowingly grabbed and took a deep breath. "Sorry?" she asked, her voice wispy and her breathing still hadn't come back to normal.

Harrison looked down at her and noticed the smile on her face. "I take it you are okay?" he asked, pulling a lock of hair gently out of her eyes.

She rolled her head back against the wall, making a keening sound. "More than okay," she told him happily. "Can we do that again?"

Sierra realized what she'd just said and her eyes snapped open. When she caught Harrison's surprised expression, she started to backtrack. "I mean…"

"No," he interrupted with a triumphant laugh. "I won't let you take that back." And he kissed her, stopping her from backing out of what he'd considered an incredible sexual experience. "But I will carry you upstairs and try that all over again, more slowly this time."

Sierra stared up at him, holding her breath. She wasn't sure she could handle that all over again! But the look in his eyes told her that she was going to like it anyway! Wrapping her arms around his neck, she smiled up at him, her body already throbbing, ready for more of the same. "Promise?" she asked softly and her body shivered when she heard him laugh in that low, sexy voice.

Chapter 8

Harrison came into his office the following morning and immediately called his lawyers and his chief financial officer in. Sitting at the table in his office, he shoved the papers towards them. "I need more information," he stated firmly. "This is all the evidence that was given to me three years ago against Richard Warner who was arrested for embezzlement, mostly of my funds."

The six men immediately started sifting through the pages. "We went through this years ago," his lead litigator, Tony, said. "We got all of your money back, plus interest from the firm. It seemed like an open and shut case."

The financial officer, a man better suited to looking at numbers than humans, shook his head. "I wasn't here at that point but this doesn't seem right," he said and pointed to a few numbers. "Plus, this looks like a report from their own accounting office." He looked up and pushed his wire-rimmed glasses higher up onto his nose. "In a situation like this, with criminal charges pending, they should have hired an outside auditing firm." He shook his head. "This is highly unusual. Why was it never audited?"

Harrison rubbed his forehead, becoming furious that he hadn't followed his instincts more closely three years ago. It had seemed like an open and shut case at the time and he'd been dealing with several major issues and a large acquisition. He'd tossed this issue over to his team and let them sort it out. He'd been satisfied that he'd gotten his money back but he should have looked into this further.

After last night's conversation with Evan as well as Patrick's visit yesterday, something just didn't feel right. And he suspected that Sierra was going to do some poking around herself and that sent cold stabs of fear into his heart. He couldn't let anything happen to Sierra. Not now. Not ever!

Bending low over the table, he braced his hands far apart and glared at the others around the table, trying to convey the urgency regarding this issue. "I want all of you to look into this, but you can't let anyone know that we're investigating. Same process applies in this review as we would take when we're looking at a target company. I want no one to know that we're investigating."

All six men nodded their heads and Harrison understood by the lights in each of their eyes that they were each thinking, coming up with ways to look into this problem. "That's all," he told them.

The men stood up and were starting to file out, already brainstorming amongst themselves. "Oh!" he said and the single word stopped them in their tracks. "Don't mention this to my wife," he warned them. "It was her father who was arrested for the embezzlement. If this comes to nothing, if your investigation only proves that he was the one who took the money, I don't want my wife hurt. She can't ever know about this, understood?"

All six men nodded their heads before moving back out of the office.

Harrison watched the men walk out, thinking that there had to be something more that he could do.

Lifting up his phone, he dialed his banker. "Bill, I need you to transfer money into my wife's account. I want her to be taken care of no matter what."

Harrison heard the man at the other end of the phone clicking on his keyboard. "Looks like you've already transferred a large sum into her account. Are you sure she needs more now?"

Harrison shook his head. "What are you talking about?" he demanded.

Bill coughed, obviously worried about irritating his biggest client. "We're talking about your wife, correct?" he verified.

"Yes. What's going on, Bill?"

Another pause, more clicking. "There's already over one million pounds in her account," he explained.

Harrison stood very still for a moment. "When did this transfer take place?" He had a very bad feeling about this.

More clicking. "It happened about an hour ago. I'm sorry, Your Grace. I should have been notified about this transfer. It didn't come in from any of the normal sources or the correct process would have been taken."

Harrison looked out his office window but he didn't see the murky Thames or the Parliament building across the street. "Okay, here's what I need you to do," he explained, and gave him very specific instructions, wanting to know exactly where the money had come from. Some of his directions to his banker were getting into a grey, legal area, but he advised the man to contact the authorities to cover his trail, but to do it in a very quiet fashion.

"I understand completely, Your Grace," Bill said, his voice filled with authority. "I will report my findings back to you in an hour."

Harrison hung up the phone and made several other calls. He knew that he had to work fast now.

Chapter 9

"Did you write any checks today?" Harrison asked as soon as he stepped into the house that evening.

Sierra turned and looked up at him, the smile of greeting fading quickly from her features. "No..." and she stopped. "Wait, yes! I wrote a check for fifteen pounds to Patrick for some cookies. But that was yesterday. Not today. It was a fundraiser for his daughter's school." She hesitated. "I'm sorry, I didn't think it would be an issue."

Harrison took her into his arms, holding her close. "A fifteen dollar check is not an issue in any way," he reassured her. She'd gone through so much over the past three years, he was damn well going to protect her from this problem. "What's for dinner?" he asked.

Sierra looked up into his blank features and knew something was going on. "I don't know. I'm sure Ruth has made something delicious, but do you have a moment before we go in to dinner?" What had happened today? Would he tell her?

"For you?" he took her hand and led her over to the sofa. "Absolutely. What's going on?"

She looked down at their fingers intertwined and her heart did a silly little flip. Don't go down that path, she told herself firmly. She'd hoped that he felt something more for her twice now and her feelings had been hurt both times when the bruising reality of his lack of feelings towards her were revealed.

She'd come to terms with her own feelings this afternoon. She'd taken a long ride on her mare and, with the wind and sunshine, the exercise had helped ease her pain and confusion. She'd also come to the conclusion that she loved this man. With every part of her, she loved him. She knew that he'd only married her to produce a child, but that was okay. He was gruff and tender, obnoxious and amazingly considerate. And she could love him with her whole heart silently.

She didn't know why, but she suspected that Harrison needed someone in his life who cared for him without reason. He had so many people surrounding him all day long, but none of them truly cared for him. They cared if he lived or died because he was the leader who had led the amazing Aimsworth Empire to such crazy heights of success. But none cared about him, the person, the man.

She did. And it was good. It was okay. She'd felt something towards him ever since she'd first set eyes on him and, with every interaction, including that first kiss, that feeling had grown stronger.

She loved him. In an odd way, it was a liberating feeling. She loved him and that was enough.

Looking up, she smiled because she realized that he'd been waiting patiently for her to speak. "Sorry," she whispered and moved closer. "I wanted to ask you questions about Patrick and…"

Harrison lifted her hand, squeezing the fingers slightly. "I don't want you to worry about that any longer. He won't be bothering you."

She shook her head. "But…I wanted to know…would other firms have done an internal review of their books after such a heavy embezzlement accusation towards one of their partners?" She looked up at him, holding her breath in the hopes that she was right.

Harrison was surprised that she'd caught onto that so quickly. It was the exact same reaction he'd had three years ago and the same comment his CFO had uttered several hours ago. "No. It isn't normal. An external auditor is supposed to review a company's books each year. There are some firms that require their accountants to take two one-week vacations each year, just to have someone different take over the employee's tasks. There are several ways that a company can ensure that their accounting is being handled correctly."

Sierra breathed out, letting go of the tension she'd been unconsciously holding in. "So is there any way to get a private accounting firm to look at the evidence that the police had against my father?" She sat up straighter. "Here's what I'm thinking," she started off. "If my father had gone to trial…"

Harrison's stomach tightened when he realized where she was going with this line of questioning. "Sierra, will you trust me to handle this?"

She shook her head. "But just last night, you said the evidence was overwhelming against my father. And this morning…"

"Just let me handle it, okay?"

Sierra looked into his eyes but didn't understand. She thought about his request for a long moment and then smiled. She loved him and with that love came trust. If he thought this was something she shouldn't worry about right now, she'd drop it. But not forever. She could concentrate on finding Daniel. That was probably more important now anyway.

"You're right," she sighed and let her shoulders fall slightly. "I'm hungry. Let's go see what Ruth cooked up for us." She stood up and waited for him to do so as well. In the end, she walked ahead of him into the dining room.

She tried to keep up her end of the conversation over a delicious dinner of braised chicken and vegetables, but her mind was working through so many details. Despite what Harrison had asked, she still couldn't relinquish the feeling that something was very wrong.

But when he took her into his arms that night and kissed her, all thoughts of her father, her mother, and even Daniel, flew out of her mind. She just couldn't think about anything when Harrison held her like this.

The following morning, she woke up, alone once again and smiled as she wondered what time Harrison actually woke up in order to be out of the house before she even opened her eyes. Right now, it was barely even dawn but his side of the bed was already cold.

She rolled over, trying to see the clock but she never was able to focus on the numbers beside the bed. Her stomach protested the movement and she had to race to the bathroom where her stomach decided to heave out whatever was left over from last night's meal.

When she was finally able to stand up again, she did so slowly. Looking at her pale features in the mirror, she tightened her grip on the countertop. Was she pregnant? Impossible! She and Harrison had been together for less than a month! How could she have gotten pregnant so quickly?

Goodness, she thought back to their honeymoon. And the weeks since. She hadn't had a period since...well, before their wedding!

"Oh no!" she thought and sat down on the bed. "Impossible!"

But she hurried to the shower, eager to get to the drugstore so that she could purchase a pregnancy test. An hour later, she had one in the bag and she raced back up the stairs, but halfway up the staircase, she had to slow down as her stomach protested any sort of hurried movement.

When she had the results in her hand, she just stared at the stick. "Impossible!" she said again. But this time, she had a smile on her face.

She was pregnant?

Already?

Harrison would be thrilled!

"I have to see Harrison!" she called out to Roger. The man was sitting in the kitchen with Ruth, reading a newspaper but as soon as he saw her excited expression, he crumpled the paper and stood up, heading towards the garage to get the car.

Jumping into the back, she rode into the city, eager to see Harrison and tell him the news. This was what he'd been working for ever since he'd come back into her life. She couldn't believe that it had happened already. Just yesterday, she'd come to the realization that she was in love with the man and now she was going to have his baby. Could life become any more wonderful?

As she walked into the lobby of his building, she had to chuckle at her thoughts. Why was it so hard for her to believe that she was pregnant? They'd had sex almost non-stop during their honeymoon. And the man was a voracious lover, never a night had passed that he hadn't made love to her at least once. It was actually amazing that she hadn't realized she was pregnant a while ago!

She stood in the elevator and realized that her breasts were tender. She had thought that was only because of Harrison's fascination with her breasts, but it must have been a sign that she was pregnant! Goodness, all of it was becoming clearer now!

"Hello, is he available?" she asked his assistant.

The woman looked up and smiled. "He's in a meeting at the moment, but I'll call and let him…"

The doors to Harrison's office opened up and both Evan and Patrick were stepping through the doors with Harrison right behind, shaking their hands.

"Glad to have you back on board, Your Grace," Patrick was saying.

Sierra couldn't believe what she was hearing. Just last night, she'd asked Harrison if it was possible that something more was going on at her father's old firm but he was here now, making deals with the men she suspected had set up her father! She had no evidence to prove that theory, but she'd thought he at least believed in her and wouldn't do business with these men.

The happy excitement she'd been feeling all morning disappeared, replaced by a cold, painful stabbing in the region of her chest. Her smile faded away just as the men turned and realized that she was there, standing in the lobby like an idiot.

She saw the look on Harrison's face and shook her head. Raising her hand, she stopped whatever he'd been about to say. "No, I didn't mean to interrupt your day. Again." Looking down, she tried to frantically come up with a valid reason for why she would be here. Other than the truth.

"I'm sorry. I just wanted to…" her mind was blank, the betrayal she was feeling too hard to overcome. "I have to go. Sorry for interrupting your day."

She stepped back onto the elevator which was thankfully still there for her. The doors closed and her last image was of Harrison's jaw clenching as she slowly disappeared.

When she was once again out on the street level, she turned to the right instead of the left where Harrison's chauffer and bodyguard was parked. She didn't want to be surrounded by evidence of his wealth right now. She was too confused, too astounded that her husband would be doing business with the men who had potentially framed her father. If what she suspected was true, Patrick had ruined her family. It hadn't been a perfect theory, but it was something and then…seeing Harrison with Evan and Patrick, she simply couldn't deal with it.

Harrison forced his mind to focus on getting these men out of his office. He couldn't do anything about Sierra or the devastated look in her eyes right now. He'd just have to trust that Roger would get her home safely.

Ten minutes later, he was furious and ready to fire anyone who got in his way. "Is everything in place?" he demanded of Bill.

The banker was quick to respond, furious that someone was using his bank to both launder money and frame an innocent woman. He couldn't even believe how simple it had been. Whoever had done this obviously hadn't expected anyone to look too deeply because the evidence was easy to discover. "Yes. The tech guys have traced everything. It all goes back to Patrick's firm, just as you suspected. We still haven't been able to dig into the other information from three years ago, but a superficial review looks like the same process was used."

"We don't have time to look into three years ago right now. I think Patrick and Evan are doing the same thing to my wife. She's in trouble. She's the priority right now." He thought about her warm, wonderful body that he'd left this morning, about the smile on her face and her soft breath last night as she'd fallen asleep in his arms.

Damn, he loved that woman, he thought. He wanted to come home to her beautiful smile every night and he didn't give a damn if he lost his title. He wanted her and if she never got pregnant, that would be okay.

He'd hurt her this morning when she'd seen him with her father's old business associates. He realized now that he should have told her last night what he was planning. But he was so used to doing things alone, of managing crises without anyone's knowledge, that bringing her into the conversation just hadn't occurred to him.

He'd also wanted to protect her. This business with Patrick was messy. Over the past twenty-four hours, the police had become involved. Detectives had been here at his office and informed Harrison that Patrick, and most likely Evan, were suspected of murdering former clients, the elderly ones, and taking control of their investments.

Harrison didn't want Sierra anywhere close to this mess.

And it was happening too fast! Something had happened last night. Patrick and Evan had built up too much wealth and today, something had tipped them off that they were under suspicion. He'd noticed it this morning during their meeting and now, with the information Bill had gathered, the pieces were both falling into place and falling apart as well.

"Where's my wife?" he demanded when he'd finally gotten Roger on the phone.

There was a pause while his chauffer and bodyguard that he'd assigned to protect Sierra hesitated. "She's in the building with you. I drove her there this morning and she seemed more excited than usual, Your Grace," the man explained. "I've been watching the doors and she hasn't come out yet."

Harrison cursed under his breath. "She left twenty minutes ago. Get with the building security. See if she left the building. And if she has, find her!"

"Yes, Your Grace," Roger replied, already running towards the building to confer with the security department.

Fifteen minutes later, Harrison was furious. Roger couldn't find any clue where she'd gone and she wasn't answering her cell phone. Rubbing a hand over his face, he tried to calm the panic that was starting to enter his thinking. He never panicked over business issues. He was always cool and calm, rising to any challenge one of his competitors tossed his way. But this was different! This was Sierra! He'd never felt this way about a woman before and he wasn't familiar with the emotions. He only knew one thing. He couldn't lose her! No way! He'd waited three years to have her and he wasn't going to let anyone hurt her now. "Okay, so she left the building. Get with the police and see if the traffic cameras caught her direction. This is very bad," he explained.

Bill and his CFO came in at that moment. "We've tracked the transfer. And you're not going to like it."

The two detectives were right behind them. "Show us," they said, their expressions grim.

Bill opened up his laptop and worked through the security barriers. When the bank information finally came onto the screen, the men all leaned forward, looking at the information available.

"I knew it," Harrison mumbled, fury rising in him that couldn't be tamped down. "Don't let her know about this," he said. "Sierra went through hell when her father was arrested. She can't know that this is all coming around again. She'll be…hurt."

She'd done so much for him over the past few weeks, he thought. He'd grown up learning to do without things like gentle touches or caring smiles. His parents had never once asked him about his day, having received updates from his nannies. But Sierra's first words when he saw her each evening was to ask about his day and she listened intently, seeming to genuinely want to know. And the way she touched him! It wasn't just the way she came alive when he made love to her. It was just a passing touch when she walked by, a kiss when she saw him. The first time she'd done it…he'd been so surprised, he'd handled it poorly and he'd hurt her feelings. But now he looked forward to leaving when she was awake, knowing that she would be there to kiss him, to care.

His phone beeped and he instantly knew that it was Sierra. Even in her anger, she knew he had a difficult meeting and she probably just sent an encouraging message.

Damn, he loved that woman.

He stood there, stunned for a long moment as that thought filtered through his mind. Love? He didn't do love. He didn't know how to love. Hell, he married her because of that ridiculous threat to his title.

A title he didn't give a damn about!

So why had he married her if he didn't care about retaining his title?

Because he loved her.

Because he'd fallen in love with her on a dark patio three years ago. He'd seen her coming alive that night. He'd seen the awareness in her eyes of how her life was not what she wanted it to be, just as he'd done with Scarlett's help decades ago.

At the time, he'd just thought they were kindred spirits but…

Ah hell, he thought. He loved her. He loved her so much that he had come up with a ridiculous excuse to force her into marriage. He'd inherited the title and all of the worn down properties but he hadn't invested any of his money into those properties because he hadn't anticipated ever living there. He'd anticipated letting the title go to his rotten cousin who was living in Amsterdam. He hadn't cared a whit for those properties. In fact, they were simply an albatross. He paid the taxes on those properties but he would be perfectly content if he never set foot in any of them again. They were piles of crumbling stones in his mind.

But if Sierra liked them, he'd restore every single one of them to their previous glory, just to make her happy. Hell, he'd buy her newer, more beautiful estates if he could just see her smile every morning and evening.

He realized that the other men here were staring at him and he chuckled. Realizing that he was in love with his wife was a pretty shocking experience apparently, if the looks on the other men's faces was any indication.

"What's the plan?" he asked, chuckling again as the happy feeling increased inside of him. Now that he was accepting his feelings for his beautiful wife, it was almost overwhelming to him.

He had a hard time focusing on what the other men were saying. But when they'd finally figured out a plan, he was in full agreement, especially since it kept Sierra out of harm's way.

"Okay, let's get this plan moving," he told everyone.

The men dispersed and he smiled as he walked over to his desk. There were several issues he needed to deal with, but his mind was focusing on protecting Sierra. He didn't want her harmed and he was now determined to figure out how Patrick had framed Sierra's father so many years ago. And why. They'd seemed to have a good partnership but something happened.

He delegated other work issues quickly and started his own investigation. He wasn't going to let this go even though he'd told Sierra just yesterday that the evidence was overwhelming against her father.

As he sifted through the data he'd gathered three years ago, he realized that the evidence was still overwhelming, but now it seemed that it was too overwhelming. It was all too convenient.

Something like that, where all the pieces fit together too easily should have been a huge red flag that something wasn't right.

He supposed at the time, he hadn't noticed that because…he leaned back in his leather chair and rubbed a hand over his face. He hadn't noticed because he wouldn't admit how strongly Sierra had affected him three years ago. He thought back to that night, her eyes staring up at him as the idiocy of her engagement hit her. He'd felt it. He'd known what she was going through as she realized what an ass Evan was. Damn, he shouldn't have let her go through this three years ago.

But he'd protected her the best way he could, making sure she had a place to live and a job. He had only hired her to exercise the horses in the stables. How she'd gotten into mucking out the stalls and cleaning out the stables, he couldn't figure out.

And no matter what time of the year or week he'd come to that house, she'd disappeared. He'd never been able to catch her again. He'd done it several times that first year after he'd bought her house, trying to find an opportunity to ask her to dinner. But she was more stealthy than he was.

"Harrison, we might have a problem," Bill stormed into his office.

Roger still hadn't come back with information on Sierra. Where was she? Harrison's mouth compressed into a grim line. "What's going on?"

Bill pushed his glasses higher onto his nose as he stared at his computer. "Well, we've frozen all of Patrick's accounts and, by now, he should know that something is going on. The investigators are in his office with the auditors and everyone but Patrick was told to clear out, just as we'd planned. No one was allowed to leave with anything except their personal belongings and all of the passwords for the personnel were changed. They can't log into their work accounts so the data is now safe."

Harrison was irritated and something in his gut was telling him that something was wrong.

The man was perspiring. Not a good sign.

"Well, we've found additional evidence."

"What sort of evidence?" Harrison snapped.

The man shrugged his shoulder slightly. "There seems to be an additional player."

Harrison's stomach clenched with a feeling that made him grab his phone. Dialing his own bodyguard quickly. "Jim, help Roger find Sierra and bring her to me here," he snapped the order quickly.

Harrison didn't want her back at the house alone. He wasn't sure why he wanted her here, just something inside of him told him that he needed to have her close by.

Sierra stared out the window of the coffee shop. Harrison hadn't said he had a meeting with Patrick and Evan but she'd known that he had a complicated meeting this morning. He'd told her that much but maybe the meeting wasn't what she'd thought it was. Maybe Harrison was just…

She had no idea actually. She wrapped her hands around the paper cup filled with herbal tea. Smiling, she thought about the life growing inside of her. She was pregnant, that much she was sure of. But maybe Harrison's meeting this morning hadn't been…maybe it was…

She sighed and her shoulders fell forward. The effort to try and justify what he'd been doing with those two men, especially after her conversation with him last night, well, it just didn't make sense.

And what about that night at the gala? She'd gotten the distinct impression that Harrison hadn't liked Evan. Harrison had had an almost physical revulsion towards the younger man. So what did the meeting this morning mean? Why had Harrison met with them?

Nothing made sense! And where was Daniel? She'd called him twice this morning and she was really getting worried. It had been several weeks without a word from him.

This morning, after discovering that she was pregnant, the world had seemed so wonderful! She'd had hope that things could work out, that her life was finally turning around. But now…she just had no idea what to think.

Roger ran past the coffee shop but stopped in a flash. The two of them stared at each other. She lifted her hand and stood up, walking out of the shop, only pausing to dump the remains of her herbal tea into the trash. "What's wrong?" she asked, looking at the man who looked frazzled.

"I need to get you back to the house, Your Grace," he said and put a hand on her arm, leading her towards the limousine that had been following him. He typed something into his cell phone but didn't say a word to her.

On the drive back to the house, she looked out the window, but she didn't notice the change in the landscape. She was too intent on trying to figure out what was going on.

Stepping into the house, she immediately went upstairs, wanting to change, put on her riding clothes. She'd just pulled her closet open when she hesitated. Was it safe to ride? Could she hurt the baby?

And then she realized that she hadn't told Harrison about the pregnancy!

She'd go back to his office, take him out to lunch and demand an explanation for what he'd been doing with Patrick and Evan this morning. Once he'd explained, and she was sure that there was a logical explanation, she'd then tell him about the baby. Her hand fluttered over her stomach, her mind reeling with the thought of a baby!

She stopped in the hallway. Goodness, she should call Harrison just to make sure he had time for lunch. Maybe he was busy. She knew he had that meeting. He was worried about it for some reason. She'd sent him a message, just a "thinking of you" message earlier when she knew he was starting the meeting. Had the difficult meeting been with Patrick and Evan? Harrison hadn't mentioned the meeting participants. Sierra sighed, thinking life was getting complicated again. And she shouldn't be bothering him at work with silly text messages.

He probably just deleted those with an irritated roll of his eyes, but she wanted him to know that she was thinking of him. Silly, but she did it anyway.

"My lady," Ruth hurried up the stairs, a bit breathless. "Roger just received a message. His Grace wants you to meet him at his office. Roger is waiting downstairs with the car."

Sierra smiled and practically clapped her hands with excitement. "That's great!" She started to head down the stairs, sensing something was very wrong. "Is everything okay?" she asked, looking at Ruth's eyes.

Ruth smiled awkwardly. "Roger is waiting. And His Grace was very insistent that you come to his office as soon as possible."

Sierra pushed the mysterious expression out of her mind for the moment. She wanted to tell Harrison the news anyway so she hurried down the stairs. Grabbing her purse, she stepped out of the front door. "Good morning, Roger. We just got back here, so do you know why there is a new urgency?"

Roger's smile was a bit reserved. "I apologize for the back and forth, Your Grace, but it is a matter of great urgency" he said and bowed but put a hand to the small of her back to hurry her into the limousine. "His Grace is waiting for you. I'll get you down there in no time."

Sierra noticed that the man was looking around the perimeter of the yard even as he closed the door quickly.

Something was going on, she thought. Both Roger and Ruth were acting strangely. She'd have to get to the bottom of their behavior, but not today. Today was all about resolving the problem of this morning and her amazing news.

As the limousine drove out the front gate, she thought she spotted…was that Evan? Why in the world was he…

No, Evan wouldn't be hiding in the trees, she thought, leaning back against the leather cushions. He wouldn't be that clandestine. He was too arrogant and conceited to hide somewhere. He considered that the world owed him everything and he was more than willing to take it.

She thought back to three years ago and she was eternally grateful that she hadn't married the man. She would have been miserable. Harrison might be arrogant, but he wasn't conceited in any way. He didn't think the world owed him anything. He went out there and conquered it. She smiled, thinking of how he'd conquered her. And she'd loved every moment of it.

Okay, so perhaps not initially. And she was still angry about him not believing in her father's innocence, not to mention meeting with Patrick and Evan earlier today. But she'd dig further into that time in her father's arrest and she'd figure out something to convince Harrison that her father was innocent. The evidence had to show her something that went wrong, something that could exonerate her father.

And she was fairly sure that Harrison knew where Daniel was and that he was somehow protecting her brother. Harrison was just too kind of a man.

Oh, she knew that he didn't love her. But that was okay. She loved him and she would love this baby. She would raise this child to be just as strong and loving and kind and generous as his father!

The limousine once again pulled up outside the massive building that housed Harrison's headquarters. She stepped out, not waiting for Roger to come around to open the door, too excited to see Harrison.

"I'll call you when I'm ready to leave," she said, almost running into the building. She caught a glimpse of Roger hurrying around, trying to catch up with her, but she couldn't wait. Harrison was waiting for her and she had some amazing news! He wasn't going to lose his title and all of his lands. He wouldn't lose everything! She'd gone through that. She wouldn't let it happen to him!

"Good morning, Your Grace," the receptionist smiled as soon as Sierra stepped through the doors.

"Hello," Sierra replied back. She opened her mouth to ask if she could get a pass to go upstairs but someone knocked into her. She looked to her right and found that Evan was next to her, his arm around her waist and something hard was pressing into her ribs.

"Ow!" she snapped at him. "Evan what are you..."

"Shut up, Sierra," he whispered into her ear. "We're both here to see Harrison," he told the receptionist.

The woman looked at the man curiously, then at Sierra. "Your Grace?" she asked, wanting confirmation.

Sierra realized that the hard thing pressing into her ribs was a gun! She nodded her head, afraid to even speak. Evan was holding a gun to her side? Had her eyes not been deceiving her back at the house?

"Were you hiding in my bushes?" she whispered to him, glad that he wasn't as tall as Harrison so he could hear her more easily.

"Yes!" he growled. "You whipped out of there pretty quickly, didn't you, doll?"

What was going on? There was a crazed look in Evan's eyes.

"Here you go," the receptionist said, handing both of them security badges.

Sierra tried to give the woman a signal that things were not okay but the woman only smiled brightly and waved them towards the elevators.

"Let's go, honey!" Evan said sarcastically and pushed her towards the bank of elevators behind the security desk.

Sierra bit her lip, trying to make some room between her ribs and the gun but he only pressed it into her side harder. "Don't piss me off, Sierra!" he snapped as the elevators opened up and they stepped inside. There were several other people who also got on and she let Evan push her to the back, trying to keep the others safe.

When the elevator emptied out on the lower floors, she turned to look at Evan who was sweating, making his chubby cheeks look even more grotesque.

"What's going on?" she asked softly, trying to soothe him as the elevator climbed to the executive floor.

He laughed. "You don't know?"

She shook her head.

"Your damn husband is interfering in things he should just leave alone."

That didn't make any sense. "Can you give me details?" she asked.

"He found out." Evan ran a hand over his face but kept the gun in her ribs. "He found out what's been going on." He shook his head. "I never should have listened to that bastard! 'It was easy money' he'd said. 'We weren't caught the last time' he'd said! 'We can just frame the bitch if she gets in the way' he'd said."

Sierra listened intently, trying to translate his words. "I'm guessing I'm the bitch?" she asked carefully, aware that Evan was dangerously nervous and that trigger could go off at any moment.

"Hell yes! You're the bitch. We took precautions! We dumped a load of money into your account, trying to get you to stop looking into the past!"

Sierra shook her head. "I'm not looking into the past," she replied. Not yet, anyway, she added but only in her head. "What's going on, Evan? Why are you pointing a gun at me? Nothing can be this bad."

He laughed maniacally again. "Tell that to your parents," he snapped. "Oh, but you can't because they died of the humiliation!"

Sierra thought that was harsh, but it was also unfortunately true. Nor was she going to argue with a man pointing a gun at her. "Evan..."

"No!" he interrupted her and she stopped speaking because he pressed the gun harder into her ribs, really hurting her now. "I'm doing the talking now!"

The elevator doors opened up and Sierra gasped when two men were now pointing their guns at the two of them. She immediately lifted her hands into the air but Evan made an obscene noise and pressed harder, causing her to cringe.

"Don't hurt her!" Harrison's voice broke through the tension.

Sierra opened her eyes and saw the furious look in Harrison's eyes. His hands were fisted by his sides and there was so much tension in his stance that she was sure he might just burst into the elevator and try to kill Evan himself. She tried to smile, tried to reassure Harrison that she was okay. Because besides the gun to her ribs, she was fine.

Harrison was beating himself up for bringing Sierra here. He'd brought her right into the mess! The receptionist in the lobby had immediately sounded the alarm and, even now, the building was being evacuated.

"Police are surrounding the building, Evan. There's no way you'll get out of here."

Obviously, Evan didn't believe him.

"Get these rent-a-cops away!" he ordered.

The "rent-a-cops" shook their heads. "Detective Alan Larson and Mike Bignall, at your service, Evan. And there's no way we can let you go. This has escalated now. Why don't you put down the gun and tell us what you know? We can make a deal."

Sierra was completely confused. "Evan, what have you done?"

"Nothing!" he yelled, pressing the gun harder. To the others with guns he yelled, "Back up and let us out of here or I'm going to shoot her and press the down button. You'll never find me."

The detectives shook their heads. "The elevators are frozen, Evan. They won't go anywhere. So why don't you step out of there and let's just talk?"

One of the detectives lowered his gun while the other backed up slightly. Sierra knew that he was only trying to get a better angle and she couldn't stop the shiver of fear that raced through her.

"Get rid of the big guy," he said, indicating Harrison.

Harrison only smiled, a lethal expression that made Evan hesitate. "Let my wife go and I'll leave. Otherwise, I'm here to stay."

Evan cackled slightly. "Hell, you're in love with her, aren't you?" He shook his head. "Don't you know that women are to be used, not loved?" He glanced at Sierra. "I could have loved you," he said and ran his sweaty cheek over hers. "Oh, the ways I could have loved you. If only your father hadn't looked into the wrong files."

Sierra looked at him out of the corner of her eye, trying not to react because she could feel Harrison's fury on her behalf. She even tried to smile, silently telling him that she was okay.

"What files?" she asked, trying to keep him talking. "Why did he look at the wrong files? I'm sure he was sorry."

Evan tightened his hold. "I wasn't even there! I came on later so there's no way these guys can pin anything on me for your father's arrest!"

Harrison stepped closer. "If that's true, then make a deal with these guys. Tell them what they need to know in order to put Patrick into prison for the rest of his life." He stepped closer again. "Patrick framed Sierra's father, didn't he?"

"Hell yes! The stupid man was getting too close! Patrick explained to Richard that it was the way things worked but Patrick wasn't going to stop."

"Because Patrick's dealings were too profitable, weren't they?"

Evan laughed again, sounding crazier by the minute. "Damn, you can't believe how much money we've made over the past few years! It's incredible! And the women! Damn, the women flock to men with money!" He chuckled as he looked at Harrison. "But then, you know all about that don't you?"

Harrison shrugged. "There are always women who will sell their bodies. It's when you find the right one, that's when the woman is worth it," he explained and his eyes flashed to Sierra.

Her heart melted with his words and she was more determined than ever that he wouldn't be hurt by this. And her father! The detectives were listening! Surely her father would be exonerated by Evan's confession!

Her eyes glanced up at Harrison again, trying to convey the message that she was okay. But he wouldn't look at her! He was focused only on Evan! Why wouldn't he look at her?!

Evan shook his head. "I'm not giving you any information," he snickered. "No way. You guys think you're so smart. But Patrick is smarter! He'll kill me or frame me if I say a word! No way!"

Harrison shook his head as well, moving forward again. "Patrick is in custody down at the police station, Evan. He's probably talking right now, making a deal with the prosecutors. And he's probably telling them that you did it all. So why don't you get your story in before him?"

That was a new twist on the situation. Evan hesitated, his eyes showing his indecision.

"Let her go, Evan. This doesn't help you. It only highlights your guilt." Harrison stepped closer. "Letting her go will prove that you're the good guy in all of this. Whatever has been happening, it's only been going on for three years with you. Patrick has been embezzling money for over a decade and we have the evidence of it. We also know that the money in Sierra's account came from Patrick's Swiss account." He paused, letting that information sink in and not looking at Sierra's startled expression. He couldn't look at her in any way

94

otherwise, the fear she was feeling would distract him. He had to get her free. That was his only thought, his only goal.

Evan's head twisted slightly, surprise in his eyes at all of that information. "You know that? You know that I've only been out of university for three years. Hell, I only interviewed for the job a few months before I met…," he glanced at Sierra and that was when Harrison moved. He grabbed Sierra's arm and yanked her forward, out of Evan's arms.

The man stood there, dumbfounded, for several moments while Harrison hugged his wife, making sure that she was whole.

"What the hell!" Evan shouted when he realized what had just happened, that his shield was now gone.

Sierra glanced behind her, not able to take her arms away from Harrison. But that was okay, because his arms were holding her tightly as well, making it hard for her to even turn around.

"You bastard!" Evan yelled. "Damn you! She was my only way out of this mess!"

Harrison shook his head. "Evan, there was absolutely no way I was letting you take my wife out of here. You had to know that."

Evan's eyes were crazy now as he moved the gun between the detectives. Additional officers were now storming the floor, some coming from the stairway and others from the elevators behind Evan. He was panicking, his gun moving around wildly.

"Just put the gun down, Evan," one of the officers stated firmly. "We can talk about this and figure out what to do next. But you have to put the gun down first."

Sierra noticed that the officers behind Evan were moving closer. Evan could feel it as well and tried to move so that a wall was at his back.

She knew the instant that Evan was going to give up. She saw it in his eyes, knew that Evan blamed Harrison, or even herself, for the position he was in now.

Her next action was pure instinct. All she knew was that she had to protect Harrison. Ripping herself out of his arms, she stepped around him just as the shot sounded. It all happened in slow motion. Sierra even wondered why the gun sounded more like a pop than a blast. On television, the guns going off always sounded like a blast.

And then there was pain! Oh goodness, the pain! It felt like her arm was on fire and she turned, looking at Harrison. His face looked stunned but her eyes moved over his body, making sure that he was still safe.

Why was Harrison rushing towards her? And why did her arm hurt so badly? Oh, goodness, why was she falling?

Her last thought was that the ceiling really shouldn't be on the floor like this.

Harrison watched as his wife's arm slowly turned red and all he could think about was getting to her, saving her somehow. His arms reached out moments before she started falling and he caught her seconds before she fell to the floor.

Paramedics were rushing into the executive lobby area and, in the back of his mind, he realized that the police now had Evan on the floor, his hands cuffed behind his back.

But Harrison didn't care. All he cared about was saving Sierra, getting her safe.

The paramedics moved in. "Sir, we need to work," they said to him but he wouldn't move. "It looks like just a flesh wound, sir, but we need to get to her quickly."

Bill moved in and put a hand on Harrison's shoulder. "Your Grace, the paramedics need space in order to help Sierra. Let them do their jobs."

Harrison heard the words and slowly lowered Sierra to the floor. But he wouldn't release her hand. His thumb stayed on her pulse. It was the only way he could ensure that she was still alive. "Save her," he ordered them weakly.

One of them pressed a gauze pad down on the wound and Sierra jerked, her eyes opening wide as the pain from the bullet wound brought her back to consciousness.

"It's okay, love," Harrison was saying to her softly, holding her hand and feeling for her pulse. "You're going to be okay. Just stay with me."

Sierra looked around. There were people moving everywhere. She heard Evan screaming out obscenities, police were stepping around her and two people with blue uniforms were doing something that really hurt her arm. And that arm already felt like it was on fire! "Pregnant," she whispered through the pain. "Don't let me lose this baby."

She knew that the hand holding hers was Harrison's and she tightened her hand as much as the pain would allow.

Harrison came into view and she saw the stunned expression in his eyes. "Surprise!" she whispered weakly.

He chuckled but she could see the stress in his eyes.

The paramedics chuckled. "We'll take care of her, sir," they said. A moment later, they moved quickly to get her onto a gurney.

"I'm coming with her to the hospital," he told the paramedics in a tone of voice that didn't allow any arguments.

Twenty minutes later, Harrison felt like he'd been gutted. Sierra was in surgery and no one was here to tell him anything.

"What's going on?" Grayson said as he stepped into the hospital waiting area.

Harrison turned, startled to see his friend. "What the hell are you doing here?" he demanded but took the man in a bear hug, grateful to have his support.

The two men slapped each other hard enough to break ribs. "I'm here in London on business. I heard that something was going on in your building and…"

Enough said. Each man had his own resources. If something was going on, they knew about it.

"Thanks for being here." Harrison ran a hand through his hair. "She took the bullet that was aimed for me," he told Grayson, shaking his head. "She stepped in the way at the last moment. It should be me in there."

Grayson was stunned. "Is she going to be okay?"

Harrison swallowed. "She's pregnant."

The two of them stood there in silence, both knowing how harmful a blood loss could be on a pregnancy.

The doors to the surgery opened up and a shorter man came through. Initially, his features looked grim and Harrison wanted to punch him. Or the wall or anything.

But then his face broke into a smile and his body relaxed.

"She's going to be fine. The bullet only hit muscle tissue, not bone. It is still going to take a while to heal."

Harrison put a hand on Grayson's shoulder, more relieved than he could even say. "And the baby?"

The doctor's smile faded somewhat as he shook his head. "We stopped the blood loss quickly, but we needed to remove the bullet. I have an obstetrician coming in to check the baby. We should know something soon."

Harrison nodded. He didn't want the baby to be hurt, but he wanted Sierra to live. And he was thrilled that she was okay.

Grayson wasn't sure what to say. "You're going to be a dad?" he finally commented, then laughed, tossing his head back. "Damn, old man. This is awesome news!"

Harrison smiled weakly. "She's going to be okay!" he said and walked over to the chairs in the waiting room. They were rough, uncomfortable chairs, but all he could think about was that Sierra was going to be okay. She was going to be okay!

A few minutes later, another doctor came out. Harrison stood up, his eyes trying to figure out what might be happening but the woman wasn't giving anything away with her expression. "Your wife is doing extremely well, despite the blood loss. We're giving her lots of fluids and I've checked the fetus' heartbeat. So far, it is strong and doesn't seem to be affected by the trauma this morning." She raised her hands when Harrison breathed a sigh of relief. "But," she cautioned, "we're going to keep her here overnight, monitor her and the baby and we'll see how both are doing in the morning. This fetus is very small. Only a few weeks old, so any sort of trauma could be a danger."

Harrison nodded his head. "Can I see her?"

The doctor smiled and nodded her head. "She's asleep now. The morning was pretty exhausting. But the nurse will show you to her room."

Harrison walked down the hallway behind the nurse and walked into the room, finding Sierra laying on the bed, her beautiful hair spread out on the pillow and looking like an angel. His angel, he thought.

His wife. His love.

Chapter 10

Sierra woke up and looked around. The room was dim but she was surrounded by flowers. They were everywhere! Goodness, where did so many flowers come from?

Her arm still felt like it was in fire, but it was also heavy. She tried to lift it but t took too much effort. All she wanted to do was close her eyes and fall back to sleep, but she didn't understand where she was.

"You're awake."

Sierra looked to the foot of the bed and there he was. He still looked furious, but she didn't understand why he would be angry with her. "Are you okay?" she asked, but the words came out as a whisper.

Harrison moved to the side of the bed, putting a hand on either side of her pillow as he glowered down at the woman. "Don't you ever do anything like that again," he commanded with absolute authority. "I will paddle your adorable bottom so hard if you ever put yourself in danger again."

She smiled slightly but then something occurred to her. "The baby?" she asked, the words croaking as the worry overwhelmed her.

Harrison put a hand to the side of her face. "So far, the baby is okay. But the obstetrician wants to keep you here, just to make sure."

"Okay," she whispered back, her shoulders relaxing again. "What time is it?" she asked.

"Around three o'clock in the morning."

She lifted her free hand to touch his cheek. "You need to get to sleep."

He shook his head. "I can't sleep."

"Why?"

"Because I keep seeing you step in the way of a bullet. It is giving me nightmares, Sierra."

"You're safe though."

He shook his head. "Don't you ever do that again!" His voice was soft because of the night, but she heard the worry in his voice.

"I couldn't let him hurt you."

He bent lower, touching his lips to hers. He'd meant to gently kiss her lips, but he felt the quiver and deepened the caress, needing to reassure her. Unfortunately the heart rate monitor started beeping faster. Not that they realized it. The only reason they were aware of that was when the nurse raced into the room.

She stopped cold when she saw the two of them kissing. Harrison lifted his head but didn't lift his hands off of the mattress. He simply turned to glare at the nurse who stammered, shocked at the two of them kissing.

"The heart rate…" she explained awkwardly. "Her heart…it was racing." She looked between the two people just as another, older and obviously more experienced nurse stepped into the room as well.

She looked at the two of them and instantly knew what was happening. "No more of that!" she told him sternly.

Sierra laughed and she felt Harrison's deep chuckle. "Yes, ma'am," he said and pushed away from the bed.

The nurses disappeared and Harrison looked down at his wife. "Why didn't you tell me you were pregnant?" he asked as he pulled a chair up closer to the bed.

Her free hand covered her stomach protectively. "I just discovered it this morning. I was on my way to tell you when Ruth relayed the message that you wanted to see me." She laughed softly. "I understand Roger's worried expression now. He was supposed to escort me into the building, wasn't he?"

"Yes," he replied grimly.

"Don't blame him, Harrison," she said and covered his hand with her own. "I rushed out of the car and into the building. It was my fault. I was just too excited to tell you."

He turned his hand over, holding hers securely. "I was terrified when the elevator doors opened up."

She heard that heart rate monitor now. It was beeping faster as she waited for him to continue. "Why were you terrified?" she asked.

Harrison sighed. "Because I love you, Sierra. And I can't stand the thought of you being hurt."

The heart rate monitor was going crazy now. The nurse came in and saw that they were just holding hands and left. "You love me?" she asked when they were once again alone.

"Completely. I love you and I can't stand to think of you not being in my life any longer. So don't you ever do anything like step in front of a bullet again."

She laughed softly, feeling lightheaded because of his words. "I will try not to. But," she licked her lips, "I love you too. I couldn't let Evan hurt you." She felt his hand squeeze hers. "I love you so much. I was just so excited to tell you the news."

He leaned over and kissed her. "As soon as you and the baby are safe, I'm wrapping you up in a blanket and you are not allowed to move for the next ten years. Understand?"

Sierra laughed softly. "Understand." She blushed as she said, "Will you be in the blanket with me?"

He groaned and leaned forward again, kissing her lips. The nurses once again came in when the heart rate monitor went nuts, but they only shook their heads and walked back out. Their patient was fine. Just in love with her handsome husband. Both women knew they should kick the man out of the room, but they also knew that he wouldn't leave. And if a kiss could do that to a woman, who were they to stop it?

Excerpt from The Russian's Runaway Bride, Book 3 in The Boarding School Series

Seven months ago....

"I'm not going to the stupid party, Mom," Livia Morgan said. She hurried through the office with her cell phone pressed to her ear, carrying the marketing designs she was going to present in a couple of hours.

Livia heard the tension in her mother's voice through the phone lines. "Please, Livia. It's just for a few hours. And your father wants you to meet someone."

Livia cringed even as she set the design packages on the conference room table and adjusted the phone so she could hear her mother more easily. "All the more reason to avoid the party. There is absolutely no way I want to meet any of Dad's cronies. They're loud, obnoxious, and disgusting – not to mention pathetic chauvinists."

Ruth Morgan didn't argue the point. There was too much evidence supporting that statement. "I hear this man is quite a catch, dear."

Livia rolled her eyes, amazed that her mother would think such a thing. Her father was a disgusting crook, not to mention a pathetic bully, and there was no way to sugar coat that fact. All of his business associates were guilty by association in her mind. "If he's in business with Dad, he's a bad guy."

"Oh, but he's not in business with your father!" her mother explained. "In fact, this man has resisted doing any work with your Dad, which is why your father wants you to be here tonight."

Livia chuckled. "Dad wants me to be the sacrificial lamb, eh?" she laughed, shaking her head as she gave a file to the copy clerk. "Fifty copies of this, please," she said with a smile.

"What are you doing, dear?" her mother asked.

Livia smothered a sigh. She loved her mother, but the woman hadn't worked a day in her life. She'd tried, but…well, things had stopped her from venturing out and getting any sort of employment. "Mother, I'm working."

Livia could "hear" her mother rubbing her forehead. "You don't need to work, darling."

They'd had this conversation many times over the past few years. "I like my job. And there is no way I am going to ask Dad for money. Never." She paused, wondering if it was time to give her mom an "out". "You know, if you'd like to come live with me, I have an extra bedroom in my apartment. You could..." could she say it? Did she dare? "You could heal, Mom. You could get out from under Dad's constant pressure and criticism. Find your own way in the world."

There was a long silence and Livia wondered if her mother was actually considering it. Ruth Morgan had been married to her father for thirty years and had taken so much abuse during that period. There had been times when her mother hadn't come out of her bedroom for days. Those were after the nights when Livia had heard her father yelling and had hidden under her bed herself, frightened of his temper, not wanting to hear the sounds.

"Goodness, look at the time!" her mother said. "I really need to hurry, dear. The party is at eight o'clock tonight. If you could be here, just for me, that would be..." she paused. "Well, that would be nice," her mother finally said.

Livia had almost made it to her cubicle when those words came through her cell phone. She leaned against the wall, closing her eyes as she heard the silent plea from her mother. "Eight o'clock," she repeated. "I'll be there, but I'm not staying long."

Her mother's shuddering breath came through the line as well. "That would be really...great."

"But will you consider my offer?" she asked, hoping that her mother might want to get out from Livia's dictatorial, abusive father. Daniel Morgan had never hit Livia, but that didn't mean that she spared any love for the man who had donated half of her DNA. Too much that had happened over the years and Livia had finally learned how to get out on her own, stand up for herself. She vowed that she would never live as her mother had lived all her married life.

"I have to run, dear. Thank you for agreeing to come tonight."

Livia hung up then, holding the cell phone to her chest as if it were her mother. She'd spoken to counselors, but there was nothing that she could do but be there for her mom, ready to act when her mother was ready to get out of the relationship.

And that was why, several hours later, she was dressed in a black, sheath dress, conservative, fake pearls at her throat and her ears as she stepped into her parents' house.

And that is also why she stopped moving, the breath knocked out of her and her body tingling with a jolt that surprised her the moment she spotted the tall, shockingly attractive man standing next to her father, looking bored and annoyed.

Until he looked across the room and saw Livia. When their eyes met, she felt dumbstruck. Never had any man stunned her like this, she thought. Even as her mother rushed over to greet her, Livia couldn't pull her eyes away from the man.

"You're here," her mother sighed with obvious relief and linked arms with her daughter. "I'm so glad. Your father has been asking about you."

That was never good. Her father's main interest in his only child was for personal gain. "Why?" Livia asked, her eyes narrowing but still staring at the man. She was trying to look away, and with monumental effort she succeeded and looked at her mother. All the while, Livia was trying to ignore the heat flushing through her because she knew that the tall man was still watching her.

Her mother's hands fluttered in the air dismissively. "Oh, remember I mentioned that there was a potentially important client your father wants you to meet?"

Livia's heart dropped, her eyes glanced towards the tall man and her heart rate picked up another hundred beats per minute when she realized that he was still looking at her. Please don't let that man, the one with the fascinating eyes, be her father's friend, she thought. Anyone else in the room – just not him! "Yes, you told me about him."

Her mother glanced around at the other guests. "Yes, well, he's been here for only about thirty minutes and already he's been making sounds about needing to leave. Your father has been trying to stall him, but now that you're here, everything will be okay."

Livia heard the panicky note in her mother's voice and looked down at her. "Is everything okay, Mom?" she asked softly, stopping their forward momentum to lay a gentle hand on her mother's shoulder. "Has Dad…"

"I'm fine," she whispered. "Just come in and meet this man. He's really quite charming." And her mother's cheeks turned an attractive shade of pink. "Well, he is in my mind. I'm hoping that you think so as well."

Livia accepted a glass of white wine, but her numb fingers couldn't seem to lift the glass to her lips. The man was still watching her, making her clumsy and awkward.

"Who is he?" she asked, surprised when the words were actually said out loud.

Her mother's startled eyes looked to her daughter's. "You don't recognize him?"

Livia shook her head, finally able to glance away. "No. Should I?"

"That's Stefan Kozlov! He's that fabulously wealthy Russian billionaire that moved his headquarters to Houston, Texas, recently. There's an enormous housing boom down there as several thousand people are relocating from all over the country. Good grief, probably the world. Everyone wants to be close to that man," she whispered with unhidden glee. "I wouldn't mind being close to him," she laughed.

Livia was so startled by her mother's statement that her shocked eyes looked at her. "Mother!" she laughed.

Her mother just shook her head and shrugged her shoulders. "Well? I'm married, not dead!" she said as an excuse.

Livia's hand covered her mouth, shocked because her mother had never spoken like this before. And certainly never about her father.

"Livia!" Her father's booming voice called out from the living room doorway, extinguishing the levity like the sun on a fog bank.

Livia turned, removing the incriminating smile from her face before she faced her father. "How are you?" she asked and almost stumbled as she realized that the tall, gorgeous man was now standing next to her father. And he was looking down at her as if she was a candy cane and he was ready to devour her. The sensation sent a spark of excitement throughout her body, despite her discomfort at being summoned by her father. Her eyes glanced up at the tall man, but she couldn't seem to actually look at him. Not when he was this close!

"Good!" her father returned with forced joviality. "I'm glad you decided to join the party," he came back, the admonishment for her tardiness apparent in his voice.

"Mom asked me to stop by, but I really..." Livia began, still intent to escape the event right after the introductions.

"Nonsense," her father interrupted before Livia could tell him that she was on her way out the door to another event. "You haven't even met Stefan."

With that, she had no alternative but to look up at the tall, devastatingly handsome man. She felt as if the world was moving in slow motion now, but perhaps it was just her nervousness at looking up at the man at close range. It had been shocking when he was across the room. But this close? She could already feel the heat of his body, sense the electricity in him.

She heard her father's words as if they were coming from a long distance, as if in a tunnel. All of her focus was on this man, on the way his dark eyes were looking into her green ones and she felt her stomach muscles tighten, her knees start to wobble. No man had ever had this effect on her and she wasn't exactly sure how to handle it. "Stefan, this is my daughter, Livia Morgan. Livia, Stefan Kozlov, from St. Petersburg, Russia."

Stefan watched the woman with the glorious, brownish-red hair and the startling green eyes look up at him. He knew she was nervous and he wanted to alleviate that nervousness, but he wasn't sure how. He'd noticed her from the moment she'd stepped into the house and thought she was a timid little thing. His eyes moved down her figure, noting the presence of full breasts underneath the black dress. But that was all he could see. The dress was shapeless, but he suspected there was a treasure beneath that material. Not too thin, full hips and full breasts, perfect curves for a man to hold onto. He suddenly realized that he preferred the softer, rounder figure on a woman versus the figure where bones were poking out in all directions. This woman would be soft and lush, definitely nice to hold onto.

"It is a pleasure to meet you, Ms. Morgan," he said and took her cold, trembling fingers in his warm grip. Lifting her hand to his mouth, she was startled by the bolt of heat that seared through her body when his lips touched her skin. They lingered his dark eyes captured her green ones and wouldn't let them go. His hand actually pulled her closer. Or had she stepped closer of her own volition?

She wasn't sure. At this moment, she wasn't sure about anything except that this man fascinated her, scared her and enticed her all at the same time.

"Why don't you take Stefan to get a fresh drink, Livia?" her father suggested. "You know where everything is."

Livia looked down at the man's drink. It didn't look as if he'd touched the amber liquid yet. Which only told her that her father was doing a bit of matchmaking. And when her father wanted something, that was bad. Romantic inclinations were foreign to her father, so if he was trying to get her together with this man, something was rotten.

"It looks as if his drink is fine," she replied to her father, lifting her gaze and challenging the older man. "And I have…"

"You work in marketing, is that correct?" Stefan interjected. He knew that this mesmerizing woman was trying to get away and he simply wasn't going to allow that. Daniel Morgan was a decent businessman. And some of his ideas were worth considering. But the entire night was now worthwhile, simply because of the man's daughter, not because of any of the proposals the loud and unpleasant man had brought up earlier.

Livia realized that he was still holding her hand when she felt him pull her forward, deftly tucking her hand under his arm and moving away from her parents. She glanced back at her mother who only smiled happily in her direction. Livia then glanced up at the man, not sure what was going on.

"Tell me about your job," he said, bringing her eyes back to his.

Livia opened her mouth to speak but the words wouldn't really come out. She tried again but then closed her mouth, feeling silly. "I'm sorry," she whispered. "If I could have my hand back, I might be able to contribute to an intelligent conversation."

Stefan was entranced. Her long, brown hair cascaded over her shoulders and down her back, the red highlights almost glowing in the dim lights of the living room. But her hair was overshadowed by her glorious eyes. Never had he seen green that color before, except perhaps on the hills of Ireland. They were mysterious and clear, shocking and soothing all at the same time.

He was completely aware that meeting her was a set up by Daniel, but at this point, he didn't care. The older man had been correct, his daughter was lovely. Now if only he could get her to relax enough, he knew that she would be stimulating company. For a few days at least. Hopefully more, but most women only held his attention for a day or two, maybe a week. They were delightful creatures, but predictable.

"Tell me about your job, Livia," he encouraged again. But his mind was wandering to what she would look like without that tedious dress on. While most women he met were draped in silks and satins that enhanced their figure, this slender little lady had chosen something that hid all of her assets. An intriguing contradiction, he thought.

Livia somehow kept herself from rolling her eyes. "My job isn't all that interesting, contrary to whatever my father might have told you."

"I doubt it. I'm always intrigued by my marketing team's ability to see through personal motives and come up with a concept that will break through to an audience's consciousness."

Livia blinked, amazed by his insight. "You do a lot of marketing?" she asked.

Stefan wanted to laugh. "You don't know who I am, do you?"

Livia saw the humor in his eyes and bristled, thinking she was missing something important. But if this man was important, her father would have explained, wouldn't he? "Of course. You're Stefan Kozlov," she replied, repeating the name her father had just given her.

Stefan watched her eyes, trying to see if she was being coy. "But you don't know anything else about me other than my name?"

Livia sighed, glancing around the man's shoulders to see her father watching them. "I know that you're a friend of my father's and that you're probably doing business with him." She glanced up at the man's hard but somehow still attractive features. "That means that you're dangerous and I won't have anything to do with you." She pulled away from him and took a deep breath. "I really need to head back home."

Stefan was so stunned by her reply that it took him a long moment to react. By the time he did, she'd already set down her wine glass and was walking towards the front door. Thankfully, it was a large house and he was able to catch up with her before she had even left the living room.

"Let's get a cup of coffee," he said and put a hand to the small of her back, ignoring her startled expression as he nudged her towards the doorway.

Livia glanced up at him, then towards the doorway and then her father's stricken expression. "No coffee," she said firmly, refusing to go anywhere with this man.

Stefan ignored her. No woman walked away from him. Especially not a woman as beautiful and mysterious as this one. She was playing him perfectly and he was enjoying the chase, he thought. It was a refreshing change from the women who were obvious in their intentions, clearly giving him the green light for a night of whatever he might desire.

This woman was much more subtle and he liked it. He realized that he missed the chase. He missed the excitement of trying to seduce a woman. And Livia was much more beautiful than most.

"We're getting coffee," he said firmly.

She'd already pulled her keys out of her purse and shook her head. "No, thank you for the offer," she replied sarcastically because he hadn't offered. He'd ordered. "I'm going home. I have an early morning meeting tomorrow and I don't have…"

Her mouth fell open as he simply plucked her keys out of her hand, tossing them to a man in a dark suit that had somehow appeared out of the shadows. "My bodyguard will drive your car. You're coming with me. We're going to talk and you're going to tell me why you don't want to have coffee with me."

Livia wasn't sure if she wanted to laugh or scream. Laughter won out but she stopped dead in her tracks, not moving another inch until this man stopped ordering her around. "Mr. Kozlov, I'm sure your employees feel very secure with this commanding routine of yours. But I will not be ordered around. I don't want to have coffee with you."

Stefan couldn't believe that he wanted to laugh. With a woman! Unheard of! He looked down at her and noticed the way she stepped back, putting more space between them. "Why not? There's obviously a connection between us."

She could deny that there was any sort of connection but she suspected that he might just challenge that assertion, prove her wrong. So she took the honest approach, facing the issue head on. She shook her head. "It doesn't matter. You're a friend of my father's, probably doing business with him. That makes you off limits."

His hazel eyes, dark orbs in the dim light coming from the porch, wouldn't release her green ones. "I am not doing business with your father."

She shivered with his earnestness as well as a large dose of fear if this man was challenging her father. "Everyone does business with my father if he wants to do business with them." Her pretty eyes turned worried as she looked up at him in the night. "He will hurt your company if you turn him down. Please don't do anything stupid. Just do what he wants and you can walk away at the end."

Stefan was stunned. And charmed! "Are you trying to protect me, Livia?" he asked, his tone gentle as his hand lifted to touch her face. He discovered that her skin was even softer than it looked.

"Yes," she replied with an urgency that she'd never felt before. Somehow, there was a sense of security, of intimacy in the darkness and this man…there was just something about him that affected her soul, touching a part deep inside of her that she'd never known existed. She'd hardened her heart to men but, somehow, this one got around all of her defenses despite the fact that she'd just met him!

The dim lights from the house softened this man's features, making him slightly more approachable, less dangerous than he'd seemed inside the house. "My father doesn't play fair, Stefan. He'll lie and cheat and do whatever he needs to in order to get you to do what he wants."

He smiled as her face turned into his hand and a surge of lust for this tiny woman hit him hard. "Please, come have a cup of coffee with me. Tell me more."

Livia stared hard at the man, wanting to both protect him and run away from him. "I can't," she whispered, but her eyes dropped to his lips.

"Can't?" he asked, moving closer. "Or won't?"

Livia's fingers curled into a fist. She hadn't realized that she was touching his chest. "Should not," she replied back, nervousness eclipsed by desire. Her eyes watched, mesmerized, as those firm, sexy lips moved closer. She couldn't believe how much she wanted this man to kiss her. How much she wanted to taste and feel those lips against hers.

When his lips finally touched hers, she gasped and pulled back slightly, her eyes snapping up to his. She was startled, not by the contact so much as the impact of that contact. But it was so wonderful, she moved in closer, standing on her toes so that she could try it again. Sure enough, just the slightest touch sent her body shivering with delight and crazy sensations.

When his mouth closed over hers, no longer willing to deal with the light, tentative touches, he took possession, kissing her with his mouth and his tongue, his teeth nibbling her lower lip until she was surprised out of her shock and forced to participate.

Slowly, as if she were in a daze, her hands crept higher along his chest while he kissed her. She felt his hands wrap around her waist, lifting her soft body against his hard one and she reveled in the feeling, moved against him to fill her mind with that amazing sensation. She heard something or someone make a strange sound, but couldn't pull away to investigate. All she wanted was more. More of this kiss, more of his touch, more of him. And she had absolutely no idea how to get it.

Stefan's hands lifted her up, pressing her against the car behind him and lost himself in the kiss. Her lips were softer than down and her body was curved in all the right places. His hands moved along her back, lifting her higher, pressing her core against his erection. When he heard her soft, sexy moan, he almost lost all control. But then he pulled back and realized where they were. Pressing this woman against a car in front of her parent's house was not the way he was going to have sex with her the first time.

Swearing softly in Russian, he lifted her back, carefully setting her feet down on the ground. He had to hold her for several moments until her eyes opened and she realized where she was once again. When those stunning green eyes finally focused, he had a hard time remembering why he'd stopped.

"Come with me," he urged, taking Livia's hand and leading her to his limousine. He had her tucked in the back before she realized what was going on.

"I am not coming with you, Mr. Kozlov," she said sternly, leaning sideways as if she could somehow get out of the limousine even though the vehicle had started moving the moment he'd closed the door.

"All evidence to the contrary," he chuckled. He liked the way her full, pouty lips were swollen and red now. She'd changed from an elegant, reserved beauty to a sexy siren and he found the change enticing. Apparently, underneath all that boring black, a passionate woman was waiting to escape.

Livia looked around, startled to realize that she really was in the back of his limousine and they were driving away. "Where are you taking me? And my car! How will I get my car? I need to work tomorrow."

Stefan took her hand, examining her fingers. She wasn't one of those spoiled, pampered women who spent her days in the salon getting her nails done. Her nails were neatly clipped, but there was no polish on them. For some reason, he liked that about her. She was clean and natural. Fresh! And incredibly sexy!

"Relax. I am not kidnapping you. I generally don't need to resort to such an effort to spend some time alone with a woman I am interested in."

Livia's eyes widened and her heart thumped so loudly, she was sure that he could hear it. "You're interested in me." It wasn't a question. "Why would a man like you be interested in a woman like me?"

His eyebrows popped up. "Because you are a beautiful woman. I find that appealing," he laughed softly. "But also because you are kind and caring. Those are qualities that I don't often run into with the women who move in my circles."

"I don't." She stared at his blank expression. "Move in your circles, that is."

He smiled slightly. "I know that. Or I would have met you by now."

She shook her head. "None of this makes any sense." She raised her hand, just trying to think things through. "Can you just drop me off at my apartment?" she asked, glancing around nervously. The intimacy of the vehicle was making her tremble. Not to mention the extremely large, amazingly attractive man next to her.

"Of course," he told her. He pressed a button and the privacy screen between the passenger and driver slid smoothly down. "What's your address?" he asked.

Livia called it out to the driver. A moment later, the screen was back in place and she was once again alone with Stefan. "Thank you," she said to him, trying to relax against the soft, leather seats. Unfortunately, it was difficult to relax around this man. He was like a live wire and she was the conduit.

"My pleasure." He watched her carefully. "Tell me more about yourself."

She shrugged. "There isn't much to tell," she replied softly.

"Tell me what there is to know. What makes Livia Morgan special?" he prompted.

Livia laughed. "I'm not special. I'm so totally un-special, it is shocking. You'd better run and hide before you find out how truly boring I am."

He chuckled, a deep sexy sound that sent reverberations throughout her whole body. "I doubt it. What do you do for a living? I know you're in marketing, but that was all your father could tell me. Or, more specifically, that was all he knew. Your father was very keen on getting us together, but he couldn't think of any details about you."

Livia ignored the comment about her father's knowledge of her life. "I work for a tyrant," she replied, looking up at him. "Probably someone similar to you. Someone who doesn't take no for an answer."

Stefan lifted a hand and ran a finger across her soft skin. "I take no for an answer." He paused, his eyes moving over her beautiful features. "When it is the right answer."

She looked up at him, transfixed by his bold gaze. "When is it right?"

He smiled slightly. "Not right now," he assured her.

They were both unaware that the limousine had stopped until the chauffer pulled the door open, startling both of them.

Stefan stepped out and held his hand to her to help her out as well. Livia ignored the hand, afraid of touching him again. His touch obviously wasn't a good idea. Better to avoid it.

"Thank you for the ride home. Even though I didn't want it." She glanced behind him. "And I appreciate your bodyguard driving my car here as well."

He almost laughed at the sarcasm that slipped into her tone. She really was a feisty one, he thought. "I'll walk you to your door."

She sighed and stepped back. "I'm guessing there isn't really any way I could tell you that I don't need you to walk me to my door, is there?" She might think he was the best looking man she'd ever run into, but he was also the most annoying. He really didn't take no for an answer, did he?

Ignoring her comment about not walking her to the door, he glanced up at the overhead light in the parking lot plus the one missing on the stairwell that made the walk to her apartment unsafe. "Not a chance," he replied, putting a hand to the small of her back and guiding her up the stairs. He turned to his bodyguard. "Go to the manager's office and ensure that these lights are fixed by morning," he told the man who immediately nodded and hurried off. Another guard stepped into the other's place, looking away but scanning the darkness.

When they were standing by her apartment door, Livia looked up at the tall man warily, worried about what might happen next. She didn't want him to kiss her again. That needed to be avoided at all costs. "Okay, I'm here. You've walked me to my door and you've sent your bodyguard off on a useless errand because there is no way that the light here in the stairway or the light out in the parking lot will be fixed by morning. But it shows that you're not a completely horrible person." She sighed and crossed her arms, pressing her purse against her body defensively. "I get it, you're trying to show that you're a nice guy. That's great. But I..."

"Unlock your door Livia," Stefan interrupted her, moving closer, knowing that it would fluster her. And also because he liked her soft, feminine scent. She smelled like cookies, he thought.

Livia pressed her back against the door when he stepped closer. "What are you doing?"

He wanted to laugh at her chagrined expression, but suppressed his amusement. She was enchanting, he thought to himself. "I'm waiting for you to unlock the door."

"I can't..."

"Give me the keys then," he told her.

She shook her head, refusing to give up her keys again. He'd already hijacked her car. That was enough for one night.

With fumbling fingers, she unlocked her apartment door quickly, then turned to face the man. "Thank you for the ride home," she said, feeling strange because he'd stolen her keys, forced her into the back seat of his limousine so she had to accept the ride and now he was crowding her in her apartment hallway.

"Invite me in for coffee," he told her, leaning a hand on either side of her head against the wall.

Livia inhaled and looked up at him. Shaking her head, she said, "No, that wouldn't be a good idea."

"Then have lunch with me tomorrow."

She smiled slightly, despite the nervousness his closeness was creating inside of her. "You're a bit relentless."

His eyes moved over her lovely features. "You have no idea."

She was starting to suspect! "I have to work tomorrow. I generally don't have time for lunch."

"Then dinner."

She shook her head. "I don't..." she stopped speaking when his finger moved over her lips, silencing her.

"Livia, we're going to see each other. Eventually, I will make love to you. How and when that happens is up in the air right now, but what is not in doubt is that I will see you again."

That finger moved over her lips, creating sensations that sparked a crazy feeling in the pit of her stomach once again. "We can't," she whispered, her stomach muscles tightening at his bald announcement that they would be intimate with each other. Oh goodness, that sounded so nice.

He smiled at the challenge she presented. She had no idea that her resistance was only making her more attractive to him. Initially, he might have thought it was all a ploy, but he suspected differently now. She was real. She was truly trying to avoid all contact with him, even though her efforts were pointless. "We will. And if you continue to refuse to see me, I will be forced into doing business with your father. So it is up to you. Only you can save me from that man's unethical clutches. Either see me tomorrow, for lunch or dinner, your choice, or I will call your father tomorrow morning and start negotiating a deal with him about some waterfront property that I want to buy and he owns."

She gasped, shaking her head. "Don't do that! It would be really horrible! You will lose so much money and he'll suck you into his horrible business world and you won't be able to get out." She didn't realize that she was grabbing hold of the lapels of his jacket in her forcefulness to keep him out of her father's business clutches.

He leaned in closer, his hand moving along her jaw, teasing the sensitive shell of her ear. "Then save me."

She started to shake her head but he kissed her neck. "I don't do business with anyone I'm personally involved with, Livia. It is a policy I have and I won't violate it. If I'm having dinner with you, then that means I have a personal relationship with your father. I can't do business with him. He will respect that."

She closed her eyes and shivered when his lips nibbled along her collar bone. "He won't respect any boundaries, Stefan. Just get out while you can. He doesn't play by the rules."

"He will. Trust me." He moved higher on her neck, his teeth teasing her earlobe. "Save me," he teased.

She pushed against his broad shoulders, her fingers discovering fascinating muscles underneath that tailored material. But she ignored that discovery, focusing only on the man and trying to keep him out of her father's clutches. "Fine," she sighed. "You win. Dinner tomorrow."

He lifted his head from her neck and covered her mouth with his lips, kissing her deeply, loving the way her hands moved up to his neck faster this time. And she pressed herself against his body instead of waiting for him to do it. She was all soft, wiggling need and he loved it!

When he pulled his mouth away, they were both breathing heavily. "Until tomorrow night, my beauty," he said and kissed her lightly one more time.

Livia slipped into her apartment, her whole body shaking, quivering with need. She leaned against her apartment doorway, taking in deep breaths, trying to get control of herself once again. But it was impossible.

If you enjoyed this preview, pre-order The Russian's Runaway Bride at your favorite retailer today! Book release will be November 20th!

List of Elizabeth Lennox Books

The Texas Tycoon's Temptation

The Royal Cordova Trilogy
Escaping a Royal Wedding
The Man's Outrageous Demands
Mistress to the Prince

The Attracelli Family Series
Never Dare a Tycoon
Falling For the Boss
Risky Negotiations
Proposal to Love
Love's Not Terrifying
Romantic Acquisition

The Billionaire's Terms: Prison Or Passion
The Sheik's Love Child
The Sheik's Unfinished Business
The Greek Tycoon's Lover
The Sheik's Sensuous Trap
The Greek's Baby Bargain
The Italian's Bedroom Deal
The Billionaire's Gamble
The Tycoon's Seduction Plan
The Sheik's Rebellious Mistress
The Sheik's Missing Bride
Blackmailed by the Billionaire
The Billionaire's Runaway Bride
The Billionaire's Elusive Lover
The Intimate, Intricate Rescue

The Sisterhood Trilogy
The Sheik's Virgin Lover
The Billionaire's Impulsive Lover
The Russian's Tender Lover
The Billionaire's Gentle Rescue

The Tycoon's Toddler Surprise
The Tycoon's Tender Triumph

The Friends Forever Series
The Sheik's Mysterious Mistress
The Duke's Willful Wife
The Tycoon's Marriage Exchange

The Sheik's Secret Twins
The Russian's Furious Fiancée
The Tycoon's Misunderstood Bride

Love By Accident Series
The Sheik's Pregnant Lover
The Sheik's Furious Bride
The Duke's Runaway Princess

The Russian's Pregnant Mistress

The Lovers Exchange Series
The Earl's Outrageous Lover
The Tycoon's Resistant Lover

The Sheik's Reluctant Lover
The Spanish Tycoon's Temptress

The Berutelli Escape
Resisting The Tycoon's Seduction
The Billionaire's Secretive Enchantress

The Big Apple Brotherhood
The Billionaire's Pregnant Lover
The Sheik's Rediscovered Lover

The Tycoon's Defiant Southern Belle

The Sheik's Dangerous Lover (Novella)

The Thorpe Brothers
His Captive Lover
His Unexpected Lover
His Secretive Lover
His Challenging Lover

The Sheik's Defiant Fiancée (Novella)
The Prince's Resistant Lover (Novella)
The Tycoon's Make-Believe Fiancée (Novella)

The Friendship Series
The Billionaire's Masquerade
The Russian's Dangerous Game
The Sheik's Beautiful Intruder

The Love and Danger Series – Romantic Mysteries
Intimate Desires
Intimate Caresses
Intimate Secrets
Intimate Whispers

The Alfieri Saga
The Italian's Passionate Return (Novella)
Her Gentle Capture
His Reluctant Lover
Her Unexpected Admirer
Her Tender Tyrant
Releasing the Billionaire's Passion (Novella)
His Expectant Lover

The Sheik's Intimate Proposition (Novella)

The Hart Sisters Trilogy
The Billionaire's Secret Marriage
The Italian's Twin Surprise
The Forbidden Russian Lover

The War, Love, and Harmony Series
Fighting with the Infuriating Prince (Novella)
Dancing with the Dangerous Prince (Novella)
The Sheik's Secret Bride
The Sheik's Angry Bride
The Sheik's Blackmailed Bride
The Sheik's Convenient Bride

The Boarding School Series – September 2015 to January 2016
The Boarding School Series Introduction
The Greek's Forgotten Wife
The Duke's Blackmailed Bride
The Russian's Runaway Bride
The Sheik's Baby Surprise
The Tycoon's Captured Heart

Made in United States
North Haven, CT
03 April 2024

50877193R10068